Take Your Best Shot

Feet of Clay Mysteries, Volume 1

Al Onia

Published by Footpeg Press, 2024.

TAKE YOUR BEST SHOT

First edition. February 21, 2024.

ISBN: 979-8224431120

Written by Al Onia.

Table of Contents

To Eldon and Sarah, who transported a green kid to Carmel
the first time

Chapter 1

Early mornings in autumn on the Pacific Coast Highway were God's encouragement for me to ride on two wheels. The cool, dense air enriched the gasoline to explode with maximum efficiency up to two thousand times per minute. The glorious chrome and metallic tank between my knees provided the energy to transport me to motorhead heaven.

The road was free from RV leviathans, either gone to the desert for the winter or not yet awake and on the trail. That was only one common distraction absent. There were still animals to watch for and deadliest of all, frost hidden in those tight turns too shaded for the dawn's sun to melt, or thawed but hidden under a greasy leaf carpet. I knew the road; I knew the spots to brake ahead of normal.

The remaining distraction was my brain. The case of the philandering dentist was nasty because he was a nasty piece of crap. I'd tell my employer, who happened to be Pops, my dad, I was through with divorce work. I had a bribe for Pops in my travel bag. Unopened 1976 Warren Zevon vinyl, a dual favorite. Pops because he was a teenager when it was released and me because I liked stuff from out of my era. Witness the Goldstar.

Another day in San Luis Obispo around Dr. James Wharton, when this two-lane asphalt heaven beckoned, might have crushed me. One more day and I might have done something stupid. Not violent, but definitely misguided.

The lure to ride had sprung me from that depression to hit the highway at Monday's first light, foregoing another All-American breakfast guaranteed to reduce my blood flow, my reaction time and my pleasure.

Instead, there was me, the bike and the road. Zen in the journey. There are three things to consider on a drive like this. I leaned into the first bend in a sunlit suite of esses. Shifting weight on the pegs and nudging the tank with alternate knees, I considered them all in a moment. First, the capabilities of the rider, in my case, mid-range. Second, the machine's capabilities, the Goldstar outmatched me there. And last, the road conditions. The track's limits, if you will. Mid-range, like me.

A single, offset motorcycle headlight crept into my bar-end mirrors. How long had it been there? The mirrors were blocked by my gloves when I leaned forward and to be honest, my eyes were on the road ahead, not behind. A fellow enthusiast on his or her crotch rocket sharing my headspace? Get on it early. If they were any kind of rider, their Japanese street-legal racer would catch me soon enough. Not a problem, I could share during the brief moment when the other bike passed. It was the journey, not the timetable. I returned my attention to the pavement to come.

Investigations also held a rule-of-three. The capabilities of the investigator. Mine were above average, I judged, or I wouldn't have the steady stream of work from clients. Even if many of them were through Pops. My dad didn't believe in nepotism for its own sake. Talent was foremost to Glen Farina. Talent and honesty. I measured up to his expectations, rarely expressed as demands.

The trees were getting thicker beside the road. The first potential ice trap was a couple of miles away. The second investigative equivalent was the capabilities of the people involved. In most cases, it was their limitations. What witnesses and suspects remembered and what they forgot. The third restraint was physical evidence. Were the clues sufficient to assemble into an accurate conclusion? Wharton wasn't careful about hiding a trail. Too easy.

A quick one-two counter-steer guided the Goldstar through a chicane I loved. Sometimes I'd go through it three or four times to get it perfect. Today I was above average and nailed it first time.

The small but intense light behind me was much closer. I resisted the temptation to twist my throttle. There was room for both of us and I'd watch its taillight shrink soon enough. Plus, I'd need to slow down in the next minute for the frosty hairpin.

I glanced in the mirror. Two helmets. Tinted face shield on the front one. Likely a male pilot judging from the shoulders and body language. The passenger's gender I couldn't determine but the matching black helmet and shield could've made them a couple.

I dropped my revs to decelerate. A blip and a downshift. The rider behind didn't pass. I moved to the right and gave him a courtesy brake light warning, feathering the pedal to slow more. He got up beside me but didn't move on. I nodded and turned my eyes back on the road. The tree-shade closed over the asphalt and I downshifted again. I'd hit my brakes hard at the right moment, tightrope walk through the frost, then gradually accelerate to dry the tires before climbing back up to full speed.

I dropped my left hand to point forward then braked. He ignored the warning and rocketed past, his passenger's right leg sticking out. Then they were down, skidding on the ice, out of it. The bike's tires grabbed the dry pavement and high-sided, flipping pilot and pillion into a spinning whirl of limbs.

"Tuck and roll," I shouted, more to myself. They couldn't hear me. I rode safely through the bend and stopped far enough away from the crashed bike that if it caught fire, mine wouldn't be in danger.

The driver rolled in the ditch, conscious and probably in pain. The passenger lay on the narrow shoulder, unmoving. I tore my helmet off and listened for vehicles approaching. I ran to the man in the ditch, wondering which question to ask first. Why didn't you follow my signal? Why did your passenger try to kick me off the road?

EMS LIFTED THE STRETCHER into the ambulance. The face shield had torn off in the crash but the medics hadn't removed the victim's helmet. I shuddered at the thought of a neck or spine injury. They'd already tubed him up.

The driver rubbed the bandage on his arm and knee through the torn leathers but otherwise seemed okay. The ambulance pulled out, siren howling. Serious injury. Why didn't the driver go with his buddy? More attached to his bike?

A tow truck lifted the scarred bike onto its deck while a kid in a safety vest picked up bits of plastic.

County Deputy Sheriff Reiger handed my license back. "Mr. Farina. I appreciate your account. We might need it in case either of them tries to press charges about the lack of signage. The locals shoot 'em full of holes as fast as we put 'em up."

I slipped my wallet back inside my jacket. "How's the pilot?"

Reiger didn't raise his eyes from his notepad. "Road rash, nothing broken. He got lucky; the ditch is softer than pavement. His passenger wasn't prepared."

"His passenger was trying to kick my bike when I braked. He missed, but the sudden change in balance and the ice put them beyond control. He was down before he could correct."

The deputy made eye contact with me. I was more interesting than his pen. "You can prove they tried to wreck you?"

I replayed the milliseconds before the crash in my head. "No. Can you give me their names?"

"You're not thinking of a little vigilante justice are you, Mr. Farina?"

I dug my wallet back out and showed him my Investigator's license. "It could be related to half a dozen recent cases and somebody looking to vigilante me. I can find out easy enough but you can save me the legwork. I promise not to take any action without talking to you first."

Reiger scribbled on a sheet and passed it to me. "You make sure you do that. We'll be in touch if we need you." He looked at the Goldstar. "Nice bike."

I put on my helmet and gloves and started up. I idled past the small crowd. I wanted a better look at the pilot without face shield and helmet but his head was down. The streaky blond hair filed in my memory.

The rest of the trip sucked. I couldn't get back into the zone. Too many questions. Too many disturbing images of the crash.

Chapter 2

Changed from road gear to casual business attire and from would-be motorcycle rocker to respectable investigator for Farina-Black and my teeth and hair brushed, I'd presented myself to the firm's namesake. Pops read my report on Linda Wharton and her unfaithful husband and all-around dickhead, James Wharton DDS, in silence. DDS for double dickhead supreme. I looked around the office for anything new. One bronze sculpture caught my eye but it wasn't new. I'd seen the horse and cowboy before, though not recently. The senior, not retired, partner of Farina-Black was rotating his objets d'art. I scanned the room again, testing if I could recognize what was new and what was missing from my last visit.

When Pops reached page three, he snorted and raised his heavy eyebrows in my direction. I shrugged but kept quiet. I knew the origin of his disdainful snort. I inserted personal opinions on occasion when an objective take wouldn't suffice. Also to elicit a snort or scoff and we both knew it. It kept the father-son dynamic from getting stale.

I continued my evaluation of our surroundings. The balance with investment services accouterments was one had to appear successful but not too ostentatious in decor. After all, it was clients' money which paid for it. They didn't mind comfort and style; they just didn't need to be non-owners of things their hard-stolen wealth had bought. A peg fell into a matching hole in my memory. A charity appreciation plaque had been replaced by this year's recognition of his fine work. It wasn't on obvious display, in a darker corner, but something he was proud of and wasn't placed to show off.

Pops finished his first run-through, then peeled back to the second page.

"Is Linda Wharton satisfied with the outcome?"

"Yes." I dug into my blazer, one always dressed up for Glen Farina, and passed him her check for services rendered, a polite term for crawling in her husband's dirt for two weeks.

He looked at it harder than my report. "This will be deposited back into her portfolio."

"Generous," I said. "Not unwise."

"Our clients need to know the firm is a life partner, not a mere service."

"Where does Clay Farina fit into the scheme?"

"You'll get paid from general funds, son. Anything you want to add, that isn't for the formal record?" He initialled the report on each page to confirm he'd read and approved it.

"One thing, it may or may not be related to Linda or her ex-husband." I told him about the tail job and the accident.

"The impression the injured biker tried to crash you, an action you could swear to?"

I pictured the leg again in the moment before they went down. "Memory's a fragile thing, Pops. I have to rely on my gut sensation at the time. I'd give it north of seventy-five percent. Fifty percent on the visual and the other twenty-five on the fact that Dr. Wharton is one king-sized prick."

"It's hard to imagine a dentist as someone who hires assassins. But then James Wharton cheated on Linda, beat up his mistress-slash-hygienist and was ripping off the health insurers." He tapped his pen on the desk, then pointed it at me. "Watch your back."

"Don't worry. Should I tell Linda?"

"No. I'll speak with her today about consolidating her assets once the divorce settlement is final. I'll hire a local man in Obispo to keep an eye on her."

"I'm impressed. Farina-Black does look out for their clientele."

Pops dug into his desktop file stack. He withdrew a dark brown folder. "I've another case for you. We'll discuss it in more detail after supper tonight, if you would join your mother and me." He passed it across the desk. "In the meantime, read up on the two cases and see what rolls out of your investigator mind. You have a meeting tomorrow here at ten. Come prepared."

"I don't like to jump to conclusions, Pops."

"I'm not looking for a conclusion. I'm looking for a way to help our client. See you at seven."

I reached into my own folder and passed him the crown jewel from my vinyl hunt down south. "For you. Zevon's 1976 album. Original, unopened. Play it like you stole it." I cracked a smile. So did Pops but it wasn't my joke. He held the album in both hands, turning to the back and then front.

"Thank you. I will play it and enjoy every note."

I endured the cubicle gauntlet and passed through the reception area, nodding to a few familiar faces. Pops was four steps behind me and I heard him greet one of the waiting guests.

"Henry, how's that leg of yours? You seem to be walking straighter every month."

"Mrs. Adams, you're here to see Milt? Stop into my office when you're done. I'd like to catch up."

Pops had a knack for remembering personal details. Or at least noting and refreshing them prior to each consultation. He was good at the glad hand and better at the investment hand.

I'd been dealt a contrary hand. My Commerce degree lay secreted in a bottom drawer of my office. Who wanted a confidential investigator who could explain demographic economics? No one I knew.

Okay, two percent of my university studies held minor interest but the rest involved computers and on those, I failed and bailed. I liked data I could touch, smell, taste and dissect, not some on-screen, so-called fact I couldn't verify beyond another screen wormhole.

I chose not to return to my Farina-Black office. The hours taken to finish, proof and print my report was sufficient cube-farm time for me today. Pops' assignment could be carried out elsewhere.

Outside, the tantalizing smells wafting from Fisherman's Wharf reminded me I hadn't eaten since last night. Breakfast willingly foregone to throw a leg over the Goldstar to ride home. Intermittent fasting kept my concentration and enjoyment keen. I scanned the lot beside Pops' building. Not sure what I was looking for, another hit squad from the mad dentist? No one lurked around my car so I crossed the street and headed toward seafood chowder and a beer before digesting the file under my arm.

WAVES SPLASHED AGAINST the pilings of The Bay Grill. As much as I wanted to sit in the sun and listen, I turned inside where my desired company would be present by eleven-thirty, rain, shine or tsunami.

Cassie Levi escorted me to Jonas' permanent booth. I glanced at my watch. Eleven o'clock. I had a half hour to review Pops' notes before my best friend arrived. "Coffee to start, please Cassie."

I began to read. The first subject was socialite Elizabeth Rudge. I remembered her case before I started to read Pops' financial details. She and ex-husband Gordon had moved in elevated circles. Gordon dabbled in housing developments and energy projects up and down the California coast. To his discredit, he also dabbled in twenty-something females. It wasn't a secret. After James Wharton's peccadilloes, I'd hoped to be free from that lowlifestyle for a month or two. No such luck. Slime marches on.

Elizabeth decided to add her feelings to the equation five years ago. After one alcohol-fuelled round of arguments, she chased him from their seaside mansion in Pebble Beach. Gordon got as far as the garage where she emptied her five-shot .22 pistol into his back.

According to Gordon, it 'hurt like hell'. He survived the shooting. Their marriage didn't. Elizabeth spent a year in the jug and three on a psychiatrist's couch before disappearing into relative obscurity.

The second profile concerned another one of Monterey's elite. Oscar Mendez had also faded from the news despite a high-profile attack on him eight months ago. The controversial developer had been shot on his way out of his home in Carmel Valley at six o'clock in the morning. Two bullets smashed through the window of his Bentley, one creasing his forehead, the other clipping a shoulder. The car fared no better. Three more .22 calibre slugs were found in the Bentley's fender. The shooter hadn't been caught as yet. Mendez's business track record, featuring four current multi-million-dollar lawsuits, was proposed by the press as motive enough. Despite his philanthropic work, the cops hadn't made or decided against making significant progress.

Mendez's father was a second-generation immigrant who'd started the family fortune rolling by brokering Mexican harvest crews from the Coachella Valley to southern Canada. He'd invested in land in Carmel Valley beginning in the 1960's and done well in developing golf course villa projects two decades later.

I noted the common features. Carmel Valley and five-shot .22's. Then I realized there was a third connection, one that was almost invisible to me and many other citizens in the area. Money. Lots of money.

My coffee was done and it was time for lunch. I beckoned Cassie. "Lighthouse Ale and chowder, please Cassie."

She was back inside two minutes with my beer and a glass of red wine.

I placed the wine opposite me. "He's not here, yet," I said.

"You're wrong, Clay."

As she smiled, I heard Jonas Mah call from the door. "It's been a taxing morning, Cassie. Make sure the next one is a 9 ounce."

Jonas slid across from me. We'd known each other since teenagers and when he moved back to Monterey from Hong Kong five years ago, we'd picked up the friendship where we left off after high school. His sojourn in the Far East had been stressful but lucrative, even under the change of control from Britain to China.

His time was now spent soaking up the sun, soaking in wine and sinking his ever-accreting fortune into an array of collector cars, all of which ran but absorbed money whether sitting still or cruising between San Francisco and Pismo Beach. He'd jumped generations from a pair of hard-working parents. His dad had owned the oddly-named Groceteria across the street from our elementary school and his mom had taught piano to a parade of modest talents, the least of which might have been me. On top of their long hours of labor, they had to raise a cowboy. Jonas was always pushing the limits.

"How was San Luis Obispo?"

"On the sundown side of middle-aged," I said. "What taxes your morning?"

"British automotive electrickery. How can you continue to ride that two-wheeled confirmation of a declining empire?"

"My Goldstar's magneto gets rebuilt regularly and I enjoy working on a single cylinder. Your Jag's V-12, I assume that's your beef, has one-hundred and forty-four more chances to go sideways than mine, if I do the exponential math correctly."

Jonas nodded. "You do but today I wonder if it shouldn't be raised to the power of three."

I scribbled on a notepad and passed him the sheet. Jonas was my fact-checker. When the facts were scarce, he had the rumor dope ready.

"Two names for you. Oscar Mendez and Elizabeth Rudge."

Cassie set my soup down. "I shouldn't pry," she said. She pointed to the note I'd passed. "Elizabeth Rudge. I can add to Jonas' intel when you two have exhausted his knowledge."

"Thanks, I'd appreciate it." I started on the soup. Cassie's significant other was a cop with Monterey County Sheriff's Department. A good one and an honest one. I would welcome her input.

"I'll assume you want what isn't in your dad's file or public knowledge. Mendez's lawsuits are closing in on him. His real estate schemes were tolerated by offshore money. Dirty money," Jonas said with a snort. "Buy commercial property high, run them into the dirt through lack of upkeep, then flip them to one of his own companies at a loss to the original investors and he'd build them back up to sell for his own exclusive profit."

I savored my soup but paid attention. "Why wouldn't offshore investors mind? Dirty money or no?"

"Because, my anachronistic two-wheel jockey, it is dirty. All to familiar to me from my time in Hong Kong, watching the desperate and rich trying to get out." Jonas tore a napkin in half, then again. "I bring you a million bucks to invest." He gave me an intense stare. "The million figure is just for doing the math. These syndicates are laundering hundreds of millions. But it's all dirty. Drugs, gambling, payoffs." He stacked his napkins. "I give you my dirty million. You lose a quarter or even half of it and I'm still left with half a mil, minimum." He wadded a napkin quarter. "A reasonable loss."

I washed down the last of the soup with the last of my beer. I wadded a second quarter, just to be pessimistic. "Seems to me you've lost half your money."

Jonas spread the remaining two quarters on the table. "The remainder is now clean. Available for more legitimate investments. Build a nest egg for the grandchildren."

"Okay, they know the risks and rewards. Isn't Oscar still taking a chance? These off shore investors didn't get filthy rich letting someone steal their money. Seems to me he's lucky to have lived this long without someone taking a shot at him. Or five."

"He got cocky. And greedy. Individual, legitimate investors pestered him to share his action. They bought the advertised line, that his empire was worth billions and growing. After a few losses, and everything was a loss to the umbrella companies, people with influence and voice started to cry foul. The lawsuits are from American, mostly Californian, investors, many who sunk life savings into buildings they thought they owned and believed were well-managed."

"How many investors are we talking here?"

Jonas shrugged. "At least a hundred. Class action suits like round, three-figure numbers."

I sat back, wiping my lips. "It leaves a lot of suspects. No wonder the cops haven't caught the assailant."

Jonas nodded. "Agreed. Even if they were motivated, the cops aren't going to run them all down. Let the courts pass final judgment. Maybe someone will confess."

"Evidence points to a non-professional shooter. Maybe an emotional one. Two hits, three misses. Or a warning." Lots to digest before tomorrow morning's meeting with Pops. I hoped he wouldn't expect too much from me at tonight's discussion. One thing I was certain, he didn't enjoy his competition playing dirty games and tarnishing the whole wealth management industry.

"Another beer, Cassie," I said. "Join us when you can." I turned back to Jonas, now inhaling his second glass of wine. "Elizabeth Rudge?" I didn't ask him to forge a connection. Without prejudice at this stage.

"She garnered a lot of sympathy when she was brought to trial. An appeal likely would have overturned her sentence but I think by that time the publicity of the case had overwhelmed her. Better to swallow two years in the bag, which became one for good behavior and her work with the other inmates. She got them reading, building skills, helping with immigration for many. A model prisoner by all rumors. Came out and retreated to a quiet life she never had with Gordon."

"What's he doing since divorce?"

"Sails his boat on the bay. Has a new wife half his age and I.Q. He golfs, she plays tennis. They drink heavily but quietly at the Santa Cruz Beach Club."

"Is he still in business?"

"No. You can break a lot of rules without destroying your business reputation but being shot by your wife and surviving isn't recommended."

I waited for Jonas to fill in the gap between names. He didn't. Cassie returned with my beer and Jonas' third glass. "Why don't you just order a bottle?" I asked

"Goes off," he said.

Cassie sat beside me. "I've got a minute. If you want more detail, drop by tomorrow night or see Dennis."

"Fill me in," I said.

"Elizabeth Rudge is now the number one suspect in the Oscar Mendez shooting," said Cassie. "Dennis and the County Herald received an anonymous tip late last night that the gun she shot her husband with was one of a pair. And she had invested in Mendez's company, Solid Gold Equity." She stood.

"Thanks for the link," I said. "You're the first one to solidify a connection. I may replace Jonas with you."

She laughed. "I don't have the liver, sorry."

"Well, isn't that a tidbit or two," Jonas observed. "One can't swing a golf club in this county without hitting someone who's done you dirty."

Or swing a leg from the back of a motorcycle. Who would take the next swing at me?

Chapter 3

Post-lunch found me tiddling my Beetle convertible inland on Carmel Valley Road. I passed the turn to Laguna Seca Park, no hot laps on the Goldie today, I'd had enough two-wheeled adrenaline rush for the day, and continued east.

Pops has photographs of Carmel Valley before the vineyards and resorts flourished. It was green, as it is now, but the housing enclaves were random gatherings of eclectic cottages. One in particular stayed in my memory. Pops and his older brother Carl posing before a concrete pillar encrusted with colored glass. Pops held a model of the lunar lander in his hands. Carl had driven them to a friend's house to watch the first moon landing on color television.

I drove past Camp Steffani Road, wondering if the pillar had survived the tear down of the original dwellings and decided not to check. Keep the image in Pops' picture intact.

Development thinned the farther I got from the coast but the estates grew larger. I found my turn-off and followed the narrow pavement strip a mile to a gated circle. Four entrances to hidden mansions were all blocked by iron and brick guardians. I looked for the moat and portcullis but I guessed security hadn't reached that level of isolation. There were no numbers. If you were here, you knew who you wanted to see. If it was an emergency, like Oscar Mendez being shot, well, it was lucky he'd been at his gate.

I pulled to the side, no doubt the subject of a camera or two. I wasn't the first outside visitor today. A cop car blocked one of the gates. From my research I knew it was Mendez's gate. The uniform stared at me from his crouched position, shook his head and waited for me to approach him.

"How the hell did you find me, Farina?" Sheriff Dennis Levi brushed gravel from his knees as he stood.

"I wasn't actually looking for you. Not here. I dropped by the station to ask you about this very case and Elizabeth Rudge. They told me you were out. I decided to check the crime scene for myself."

Dennis had four inches and forty pounds on me. Those forty and the other hundred and sixty were all in better shape than my mass of tissue and bone. His straw hair and tan made him look like a surfer, which he was in his spare time. "You better fill me in," he said.

"I'm on the Elizabeth Rudge side. can tell you a bit but the rest is murky to me until Pops fills me in. I was querying Jonas about Mendez and Rudge after Pops passed on notes regarding both for my review before a meeting tomorrow. Cassie saw Rudge's name and said you were the one to receive a tip." I looked around at country and lifestyle more suited to my parents than me. "Great day for a drive and thought I'd get a view of Mendez's attack for myself. Were you on the original case?"

Dennis shook his head. "No. It passed through a few hands before reaching the 'ongoing but inactive pending more information' stage."

I walked to the pillar anchoring Mendez's gate to study the mechanism. "They open inward," I said. "Significant?"

Dennis shrugged. "I don't know. Yet. More convenient when you're coming in at night, I suppose. Exiting takes longer but who's in a hurry to leave a place like this?"

"The shooter waited where?"

Dennis pointed to the main entrance. "Back there, the camera is recent but would be out of range regardless. Gate opens. Gives the attacker plenty of time to leave their vehicle, trot over to Mendez's car while he's waiting for the gate to allow exit. A person on foot easily squeezes the narrow gap. Fires through the window before Mendez can move. Runs back to their car," he pointed again, "and gone."

"Video?"

"Hooded jumpsuit. Height and rough build from the scale of Mendez's Bentley. Nothing on the escape vehicle, not even tire marks."

"Elizabeth Rudge's name surfaces eight months later, given the similarity of weapon. I would think .22 pistols are a delete option in this area."

Dennis grinned. "Don't bother with the cigarette lighter but I'll take the glovebox ordnance. I hear you. But there's another piece."

He hesitated. "You don't have to compromise your job, Dennis. I'll find out in good time."

"No, this will come from your dad anyway. Elizabeth Rudge was one of Mendez's victims."

"How much?"

"Her divorce settlement came to five mil. Half of it more or less liquid, half of it tied up with Mendez. The ex's assets were all in Mendez, thought he was pulling a fast one on the courts. Do the math for Elizabeth."

"Two point five million." I looked past the gate. Mendez didn't seem to have hit the skids. "Shit."

"Exactly."

CARMEL VILLAGE POST-school dismissal gridlock was in full swing. Upscale SUVs engaged in a puzzle with no solution other than time. I followed in Dennis' wake. He blipped his siren once to clear a double-parker outside the Bean There Done That coffeehouse and parked in a red zone. I wadded behind him. "Does your official jurisdiction cover me?"

"I'll watch," said Dennis.

We sat outside, enjoying the late afternoon sun.

"Have you met Mendez?" I asked.

"No. I keep our investments in a sock drawer."

"I've sunk mine into British Cycle Repair. Although I haven't taken an equity position. I probably should if I hang on to the Goldstar much longer." Which reminded me of a second subject to broach before Dennis left.

"Was Cassie right? Do you have a fresh link?"

Dennis frowned. I hoped I hadn't got Cassie in trouble.

"Yeah, I do. A tip. Not a secret given the other recipients."

"What can you share?" I sipped, grimaced and added sweetener. I'm a heathen.

"Text message received on Sunday. It originated from a prepaid phone bought from a wharf vendor over a month ago. The seller doesn't recall the buyer. Snowbirds buy them in bulk, usually cheaper than their own long-distance plans."

"You answered most of my questions. The message?"

He fiddled with his phone and passed it to me. The suddenly blank screen was another mystery. One I didn't care to solve. I swung it around. "Please. One for the luddite in me."

"Right." Dennis' finger blurred across the screen and he spun it.

Mendez and Gordon Rudge shot with similar gun. Coincidence or habit? Check Mrs. Rudge's loss thanks to Mendez. Maybe she isn't cured.

"Not much. Didn't these links come up in the initial investigation?"

"Her name wasn't in any of the class-action suits. That part's new. The weapon? As you said, ubiquitous." Dennis eyed the street. "I could find half a dozen within a few blocks."

"What's this mean at the top?" I touched the screen, causing it to dance to another menu.

"One of the other recipients. The number is Elizabeth Rudge's landline. She would have got a computer-voiced version."

"That'd be spooky. When did she call you?"

Dennis nodded and chewed his pastry. "Last night. In fact, I heard from another recipient almost the same time."

"Who?"

"Colin Marsh, reporter for the County Herald got a printed version. Apparently, the paper's phone lines were down."

The image of a linebacker-sized man jigged me. "I've met him. He covers the Concours d'Elegance. Pops and I chatted with him the year they did motorcycles. He's not on the crime beat."

"No, he isn't. What he is on is the social circuit. Mendez and the Rudges are well-known to him. Despite their peccadilloes, they are philanthropists. At least Mendez still is."

I swept the remaining bitterness from the coffee away with a raspberry tart. "Different angle. You cover the crime side, Colin the social. Any thoughts on the motive for the tip? A frame? A grudge? The real deal?"

"I can't say. Any and all of the above. Gordon Rudge, just to inconvenience her. Hell, could've come from Mendez himself, frustrated at the lack of progress."

"I think Pops wants me to meet Mendez tomorrow morning. I'll suss him out and tell you my impressions." Then I realized another possibility.

Dennis moved his chair back. "Appreciate it. I'll have to talk to him soon as well. Query him about Elizabeth Rudge. See if he knows her or the ex."

"Before you go, one more thing. I witnessed an accident this morning on my way up the coast. You may get the report from Deputy Reiger. If you do, can you run a check on the names? It was another bike, following me or chasing me, not sure. I think the passenger tried to wreck me and missed. They hit frost and highsided. The passenger was pretty messed up."

"Why would anyone be after you?"

"It could be related to a case I finished for Pops in San Luis Obispo. Some people resent being caught."

We both stood. "I'll watch for the report through the traffic division."

"What did Elizabeth Rudge say about the tip, aside from her shock?"

We walked to our rides. "I didn't push it. Sheriff Marx talked to her lawyer first thing this morning. She and her counsel are aware we'll be following up. The kid gloves are on unless we get more than a poison pen note. She served her time. She had public sympathy on her side. We're not in the business of shattering a new life it's taken years to assemble, free from guilt and shame."

"You folks are human after all," I said.

"Sometimes."

"See you around, Dennis. And thanks."

Chapter 4

Mother and Pops' house sent the same message as his business; prosperous but a lap short of over-the-top ostentation. The gate was the only external hint that something lurked inside worth protecting. I'd convinced him to install it. Protecting valuables? One minor reason. Protecting against vandalism which was more distressing. Encourage would-be thieves to move on to easier pickings. It was also about personal safety. You never knew when a client might take a market setback the wrong way and start looking for an easy target. Witness the leaking Mendez.

I drove through and parked behind an unfamiliar Westfalia campervan. The Cal State parking decal suggested a colleague of mother's. A side rack for a kayak almost clipped me in the head. *Hang a ribbon for tunnel visionaries like me*. The smell of barbequing fish hastened my pace.

The rear patio held no party. Just the folks and one guest. The ponytail revealed gender. Another fixup? Thanks mom but give it up. I like to choose my own female company. I put on my suave smile and gritted my teeth.

"Clay," mother called. "Bar's there." She pointed.

The ponytail turned to face me and my teeth unclenched. She was younger than me, five years maybe, clothed in an intricately embroidered dress. Her hair and skin were dark honey. She exuded casual charm, not easy to pull off. Mother, your taste improves. I grabbed a cold beer, it being the quickest fix, and continued toward the group. Pops was behind the two women. He grinned like an idiot then shrugged his shoulders.

I kissed mother, put my beer down, wiped my hand dry and smiled at the stranger in my midst. "Clay Farina." I beat mother to the punch. Having her introduce me as 'sonny' or 'junior' wouldn't do. I was thirty years old and could tie my shoes most days.

"Ynez Jones."

Her grip was firm. The kayak was no hobby, I guessed, it was a lifestyle.

"Ynez joined the Environmental Studies faculty in September," mother explained. "One of my unofficial roles includes orienting new instructors as well as students."

I finally untied my tongue. "Environmental studies. You focus on the ocean, right?"

"Not just the ocean. I went to school in Santa Barbara, you can't miss the Pacific. It's on the left."

Smart and funny. I chuckled appropriately.

"Getting on the water got me through a lot of doctorate stress. I'm teaching the intro course so I'm a bit all over right now. Your mom's teaching statistics to first year students so we crossed paths."

My mother was the Assistant Dean of Mathematics, her teaching duties normally consisted of fourth year seminars to wanna-be graduate candidates.

"I drew the short straw," mother explained.

Pops fussed on the grill.

"I drove past Camp Steffani this afternoon," I told him. "I didn't go in but thought of your old picture with you and Carl."

He finished his culinary task and sat with us. "There were four of us that day. Carl and I thought about trying to get the guys together on the Armstrong landing's fiftieth anniversary for an updated shot but Carter's up north and Wyatt's a drunk. I don't have much in common with either of them anymore. Why were you there?"

"I thought I should take a look at Mendez's place before the meeting tomorrow."

He subtly pointed his glass toward the ladies. "Your mother's guest calls for a change in plans, no business tonight," he said. "Except teaching gossip. We'll brief in the morning. Come early."

Fine by me. Our conversation was more interesting than another case. Ms. Jones held more fascination than I could muster from my side. Her passion for her work and desire to imbue it in her students was as she put it, 'the best lesson I can give'.

Touché compared to my field. I didn't even have a real field I could go stand in or kneel upon to study the critters below. Her ideas of a confidential investigator's life seemed limited to television studs. I admitted I'd once driven off a pier chasing a suspect. I was on a bicycle and he was on a skateboard. And we both were eleven. Cue the theme music.

I stopped at one beer and two salmon steaks. There was no way I wanted to bunk in at the folks' my first night home in two weeks.

I walked Ynez to her van on the excuse I had blocked her in. "I don't always welcome parental intrusion into my personal life," I began, "but I appreciate my mother's gesture to welcome you to the bay area. Tonight, I won."

Ynez leaned against her van, arms crossed but not in a conscious body-language pose. "I did too. You don't have to pursue it further if you don't want to."

"I think we'd best give it one more engagement before I call off any pursuit. Dinner in the next week?"

"That's pretty wide open, Clay. You'd best up your game."

Ynez Jones would not be taken for granted. "You're right. Sorry, I'm a bit rusty. Saturday. I'll meet you at Spinnakers on the Wharf. Six or seven? See, I'm not entirely arbitrary."

"Seven it is." She gave my hand a squeeze and climbed into the van.

I listened to the four-banger rattle and pop before settling down to an uneven cough. If we consummated my pursuit, I'd need to hook her up with my mechanic and sort the Vee-Dub out.

I backed out the beetle, watched her leave and then trundled home to Pacific Grove. I tried to forget the day's mass of stimuli. It didn't take and I had a crappy sleep. At two a.m. I was awake, reliving the bike crash. At three, I arose and read Pops' files for real, instead of the virtual scan I'd been repeating in bed.

By four, I was ready for a nap. It succeeded and the 8 o'clock alarm was distinctly unwelcome.

Chapter 5

Monday's County Herald had been printed twelve hours later than usual and was a day late on the newsstand. I bought it on my way to a sidewalk breakfast. Breaking News Investigation by Colin Marsh had stopped the presses screamed the bold headline. Colin Marsh's story regarding the Mendez shooting case's revival made the front page.

I read while I ate in the morning sun. Hattie's Bistro coffee'd and fed my tummy. The sun's rays fed my soul.

The opening paragraph was pure purple. "A foggy February morning like any other in the Carmel Valley hid danger. Out of the mist crept a would-be assassin, waiting for the precise moment to empty a handgun into the car and body belonging to Oscar Mendez. The well-known businessman survived but the attacker vanished back into the dawn's haze." After this flowery beginning, Marsh did his journalistic duty in reporting the tip and questioned every statement. He questioned the time lag between shootings with regard to Elizabeth Rudge's involvement in the second. He didn't know or hadn't reported that she was connected to Oscar through one of his shell companies and had ripped her off, along with many others. A good reporter would have. A financially astute newspaper employee would save it for a follow-up feature. And there it was at the end. Read Wednesday's paper for the rest of the story; where the police investigation stood before this latest news and how Mendez and Rudge might be connected.

I finished up and returned to my condo to don a sport jacket for my meeting at Farina-Black. I slipped the newspaper in with Pops' file and drove.

With ten minutes to spare upon arrival, I picked up my check for the previous case and sat outside the conference room beside Pops' office. I heard voices inside. One was Pops', even through the door his inflections were second nature to me. The other two were too muffled to recognize beyond one male and one female. Was the male Mendez? Audrey Ellis wasn't in her office. She could be the third. I folded the newspaper to cover the story and tucked it in my jacket.

Pops came out, closed the conference door and sat down beside me. "Morning. Mom asked me to pry."

"Ynez and I will dine Saturday evening. Don't call and don't join us."

"I'll tell her you have made plans, nothing more," said Pops. "Now, I hope you haven't made too many preconceptions surrounding the profiles I gave you."

I took out the paper. "I've read this, not much to assume about Marsh's article. I spoke with Jonas; he comes down hard on Mendez. Tell me it's unjustified, that the higher the promised return, the greater the risk, knowledgeable investor and all that, and I'll reserve final judgment. At least until I meet Mendez and he creates a better impression than the general consensus."

"I've met him numerous times. He is whatever he wants you to think he is. The man is a context chameleon."

"Am I meeting him now? I heard at least one voice in there." I pointed to the door.

"Roger Schopff."

"The lawyer? Good call, I might need him after yesterday's road encounter."

"How is the rider?"

"I don't know," I said. "If I have time, I'll visit the hospital after this."

"Do it. Then get on with this new inquiry."

"Who's the other guest?" I was spinning the same record.

"Elizabeth Rudge. Schopff is her lawyer. I'd put the newspaper away. She's seen enough this morning. Your initial thoughts?"

I shuffled my prepared summary of Mendez to Mrs. Rudge. "The soap opera life with Gordon was toxic. They seemed to revel in elevated social circles but didn't hold back their mutual animosity in such gatherings. Did she grow up rich and snooty?"

"Rich, yes. Entitled more than snobbish, I'd say. Gordon didn't start at the same level. He clawed his way up."

"Legitimately?"

"He had charm and intelligence," said Pops. "Gordon was not a risk-averse personality. He was the kind of man mothers warn their daughters to avoid. To Elizabeth, he was a chance to break free from the restrictive social set her parents chose."

"She got what she wanted. Did she deserve it?"

"Time for you to meet her and decide for yourself."

We entered together through the double doors. Schopff rose to greet me. Elizabeth Rudge was older than the photo on page one. She was trying hard to stay composed but worry lined her face.

Pops handled the introductions and we all took coffee to establish a shred of normalcy. He explained my presence. Something I wanted to learn myself.

"Clay is Farina-Black's confidential investigator." Pops turned to Elizabeth directly. "You are my friend and my client. My services and therefore, his, are yours. Roger, perhaps you can summarize our options going forward, in light of the allegations made to Mr. Marsh and the police."

Schopff said, "I'll answer Clay's obvious question before I go on." He was suddenly the humble, back-woods, aw-shucks mouthpiece. "How can Elizabeth be a well-heeled client of your fathers' firm and Mr. Mendez's victim?"

"Good guess." I had to give him credit. She was better fixed than I thought. Money to burn; or in this case, pass it onto Mendez to burn.

Elizabeth spoke. Her voice was a deep contralto and the shakes had gone. "I placed my parents' inheritance with Farina-Black and going back fifteen years, continued to add to my portfolio as the situation permitted. Gordon, my ex-husband, may he live in torment, chose to invest a large sum into three Mendez companies before the divorce settlement. Half of my settlement was more liquid, thank goodness, but I watched the rest circle the drain. I was in custody and foolishly agreed to the terms. My consolation is that he lost a pile too."

Schopff picked up the narrative. "This new rumor places Elizabeth in a defensive position once again. The publicity will spur the police to actually try for a resolution, something I doubt was at the front of their caseloads. If any case involving Elizabeth proceeds, and I don't think it will go that far, but if it does, the district attorney's office will look for motive, opportunity and state-of-mind." Roger counted the factors off on three fingers. "Elizabeth and I discussed the scenarios before you joined us but I will elaborate for you."

"Thanks," I said. And where do I come in again where I don't cross the police?

"First, motive. Easy to establish. Elizabeth's losses amounted in the seven figures." Schopff tapped his finger on the table. "Opportunity. A murky area. Providing an alibi this long after Mendez's shooting could be problematic and I wouldn't want to rely on witness memories. I'd be able to cast more than reasonable question upon any were I cross-examining. Prove beyond reasonable doubt she did it. We're solid there, in my opinion." He paused.

"Sounds like that would still constitute a risk," I said.

Schopff nodded. "I'd be swimming hard." He finished tapping and nested fingers together. "The best defense is not having to defend."

Now I got it. I glanced at Pops. He gave me a quick nod of congratulations. His faith in his son confirmed.

Schopff finished. "Prove beyond a reasonable doubt that someone else shot Oscar Mendez."

There it was. Throw Clay in front of the police bus. A chance to act on my distaste for Mendez and his ilk. "Is this how you'd like me to proceed, Mrs. Rudge?"

"Yes. Please call me Elizabeth. I was Mrs. Rudge for so long, I haven't quite gotten ready to change to my maiden name, despite my loathing for the association with Gordon."

Schopff and Elizabeth stood. We all shook hands again.

"I will need to speak with you both in more depth," I said.

Elizabeth handed me a card with a Monterey address and phone number. "Call me tomorrow morning and we'll set a time."

Schopff passed me his card as well. "Set it up with my office, Clay. I want you to get your feet wet first, then we'll have more to chew." He escorted Elizabeth from the room.

I stayed behind. "You surprised me, Pops. I thought I'd be meeting Mendez, not her."

"I would prefer he not set foot inside Farina-Black. His type gives us all a bad name. He makes it worse by building up a public benefactor persona, and complicates opinion by performing a lot of solid, honest charity."

"It's hard to understand the dual role. Unless one of them is completely wrong. Is there a chance his investment shells have run into bad luck? Bad timing? A bigger scammer?"

Pops swivelled in his chair. "Zero chance. The man's an economic sociopath."

"Why hasn't he been shut down? The Securities Commission can't ignore the lawsuits, can they?"

"They don't ignore him but they do a kind of financial triage. Staffing, resources, ranking priorities. They'll get to him eventually. The civil class-action suits are a blessing for the Attorney General's office. The negative publicity will scare off potential clients so they don't have to petition for a ban, which might be all they could do anyway. A hefty fine would take away from any recompense awarded to the investors. It's a wait and see."

"I'd like to meet him. Get a personal impression. I don't like to rely on second or third hand conclusions."

Pops spoke into the intercom on the conference table. "Milt? It's Glen."

"Hi boss."

"Can you dig out the details on the Recent Immigrant Fundraiser and Auction this Saturday and bring it in to the conference room. Thanks."

Pops explained. "One of Mendez's higher profile charities. Funnels the money raised into tutoring for immigrant kids. ESL in particular. He has a committee struck to ferret out the smartest kids and sets up bursaries for them and extra education."

"Sounds long term," I said. "And pretty decent."

"I agree. The two sides of his coin, so to speak."

"How long have you known about Mendez's schemes?"

Pops reclined to gaze at the ceiling. "Two, three years. We had clients who wanted to shift funds into his real estate investments offering a criminal rate-of-return. The old adage, 'if it seems too good to be true, it isn't true' was good enough for some, insufficient for others who bought in, then came back to us looking to increase our level of risk to recover their loss."

"It must have taken some self-control not to use the other 'I told you so' adage."

Pops shook his head. "That isn't how Farina-Black operates. We worked out a revised, realistic end game and adjusted their portfolios to attain same."

"They still had to be pissed, though." Pissed enough to point and shoot.

"For a few, lifestyle changes were in order and that's the hardest part."

"Can I get a list of those hardest hit? The ones whose lifestyle changes ground them the most?"

"I'd be compromising confidentiality."

"You heard Roger, the best defense for Elizabeth is to provide a genuine suspect. Someone who might decide you're not living up to their expectations for a luxury retirement." I gave him my most innocent look. "I won't embarrass or implicate you."

"I'll give it thought," said Pops.

A knock and the doors opened to admit Milt Canyon, one of the firm's long-timers. He nodded toward me. "Clay, good to see you."

"Likewise."

"Here's the announcement and tickets. We bought ten."

Pops scanned the list then looked up at Milt. "Who'd appreciate being bumped?"

"Besides me? Daly and his wife just had a grandchild. They'd prefer to send a check."

"Good. Give Clay their tickets."

"I'll ensure the final guestlist includes him."

"Thanks, Milt."

He waved on his way out. "See you there, Clay."

"You will take a guest," said Pops. "How about Ynez?"

"She might get the wrong idea about my financial status. Do I have to bid on anything?"

"Not competitively. Let her see what you write on a few of the silent auction bid sheets."

"Anything else?" I would have to have my tux cleaned to at least blend in visually.

"No. I'm sure you have enough to start."

"I'll be back for your list tomorrow." Time to begin my own list of avenues to pursue in the meantime. Simple. Find the attacker eight months after the fact. Clear Elizabeth Rudge. Squire Ynez Jones. First item. Talk to Colin Marsh and find out why he was the recipient of the tip-off.

Chapter 6

The County Herald's news office was less than I expected. My vision of rows of desks with clattering typewriters and a cigar-smoking editor in suspenders and shirtsleeve bands screaming 'copyboy' were locked in a film noir impression. Two empty desks with computers on top guarded the lone interior office. The plastic tag beside that door read 'Felicia Diaz, Editor'.

I knocked and looked in. A fifty-ish woman peered over the tops of her reading glasses.

"Hi. How can I help you?"

I took a step. "Clay Farina. I'm looking for Colin Marsh." I looked over my shoulder at the empty newspen. "I guess he works from home?"

"Everybody does, most of the time. Except me." The phone rang. "Come and sit down." She gestured to the chair beside her control center.

She picked up the phone on the fourth ring. "County Herald, Diaz here." She scribbled on a notepad while making confirmation noises. "Got it. Thank you for calling." She hung up and looked at me. "Farina. Any relation to Wendy Farina?"

"My mother. Do you know her?"

"I do." She didn't elaborate.

"And dad?" Find out which social circles Felicia occupied.

"No, I don't think I've met him. Glen, right? Wealth management. Managing my 'wealth' isn't currently causing me stress. Tell your kids, if you have any, that if they want to be free from financial worry, pursue a news career. You won't have significant finances to worry about." Her laugh was genuine and got me smiling.

"If and when I do extend the family tree, I will remember."

"You wanted to see Marsh. Why?" She still had the pen in her hand.

"About his tip on the Mendez case."

"Go on."

"Not sure how much I want to tell you, no disrespect. I'd prefer to keep it off the record." I stared at the hovering pen.

She dropped it and leaned back in her chair. "What do you do, Clay Farina?"

"I am a consulting investigator. At the moment I am engaged by my father's firm to lend my service to their client, Elizabeth Rudge. The accused." I pulled out the morning's paper.

"There are times in my position where I have to put aside personal convictions to serve what the fifth estate thinks is the greater good," she recited. "Information."

How much of the rote did she believe? "It seems to me, there isn't a whole lot of straight information in this article. It takes an unfounded accusation and brings two citizens back into the public eye which might not be what they, as part of your public, desired."

"Mr. Farina, you're not going to win a moral high-ground argument with the news. Everything is news. The phone call? Whale carcass spotted outside the bay. Fourth one this year. Still news. Comes to us. That caller has cellphone video. I don't even need to send someone out on the water. The tipster can talk to me or one of my stringers and Mrs. Rudge and Mr. Mendez will be replaced on page one tomorrow by a dead cetacean."

"You'll divvy up the information to cover a few days editions, just in case the next page one doesn't fall into your lap. What happened to investigative journalism?"

She rested her elbows on her desk. "Time, money and readership. Sure, the public still wants to learn but they want something to stir the blood."

"Really? I can't tell you how many times I've listened to or read a story and wondered where were the tough questions. You could fill a weekly special issue with resolution for all the half-finished stories."

"We give stories which have an ending, eventually. We're in business to sell papers, specifically, the next edition."

The street door opened and a male voice called. "Felicia?"

"You're in luck, Clay. That's Marsh."

A sturdy, sandy-haired guy I recognized stuck his head in the door. The goatee was new. He held up page one and asked, "Was this really the most recent picture we had for Rudge?" He noticed me. "Hi." Marsh turned back to his editor.

"Yes, your old social page group shots were too blurred and my only other option was her booking photo." She introduced me. "Meet Rudge's private eye. Talk out there, I've a whale of story to log."

"Thanks for your time and thoughts," I said. "We'll chat again."

"We may, Mr. Farina. Your mother's a great lady. If you're a fraction, you're worthy of my time. Despite your uneconomic views on reporting."

Marsh closed the door and we stood in the front office.

"Had lunch?" I asked.

"Are you buying?" He gave me an appraising squint.

"I am if you like The Bay Grill."

His scrutiny evaporated.

As we walked toward the pier district, I mentioned his past coverage of the Concours d'Elegance and then explained my role for Mrs. Rudge in brief. He didn't run away so I let him get settled in a booth and ordered before the questions.

"I'd like to hear how your tip about Mendez came in. Phone, email, note slipped under your door? Rock through a window?"

"Never had one under the door, but then I'm not covering the hot topics. Crime, environment, elections. I get the fluff." Marsh didn't crack a smile. "Fluff which sells papers."

I flattened the morning's paper on the table. "You're a good writer. Left me wanting more." I didn't a crack a smile either. We were both tough guys. "Is there any more?"

He held my gaze as the breakfast-lunch server set down water for me and diet cola for him. Then he grinned. "Not much. But I've got the rest of the day to find out."

"Tell me what you have and I'll buy two papers tomorrow. Double the Herald's circulation."

"Some day you'll pay me back. The Farinas are plugged into the upper echelon in this area."

"No promises. My parents' privacy is important. After the ball is over."

"No problem. I need to confirm the allegation Elizabeth Rudge was one of Mendez's victims. The gun she used on her ex-husband was put into an evidence tomb and has likely been destroyed by now. But I'll confirm. I'll check with the business reporter on the current status of Mendez's suits. I can stretch it out another week if I try hard."

Our sandwiches arrived. I let him finish his first mouthfuls before I prodded. "You still haven't told me how you got the tip. And speculate why it was you?"

"Not just me. The cops got the same tip, different format. Mine was a printed note."

"You have it with you?"

"Only a copy. If you want forensics on the original, I suggest you talk to the cops. To me, it looked like a piece of common paper and font."

I read it closely. It matched Dennis' text word-for-word. I washed down my food. "It was easier forty-plus years ago when people used typewriters. Like fingerprints, they say. You just had to find the matching machine. Course that wouldn't be easy if you had fifty machines to check. Why you?"

Colin shook his head. "I don't know. Maybe the source met me one time and thought I'd act on it quickly."

"Publicize it first, fact check later."

"Nothing in this is wrong, Clay." He tapped the newspaper.

"Granted," I said. "It doesn't help Elizabeth Rudge in her quest for anonymity. Do you think your source is just trying to hurt her? I mean just because she had the stones to plug her husband after a night's heavy drinking, doesn't mean she would plan and carry out a strategic strike against Mendez."

"People can surprise you. Grudges last."

I shook my head "I met her this morning. She seemed overwhelmed by this."

"I've met her too. Years ago, when she and Gordon still ran with the big crowd. She reveled the lifestyle and tolerated his dalliances. I was surprised when she shot him. Not that they didn't have the odd tiff in public, but I guess she had a tipping point."

God, I hated that phrase. It's like everyone and everything balances on a knife edge. The thought of one day all the tips simultaneously breaching is apocalyptic. Did someone else in Elizabeth's world have a tipping point? Roger Schopff had missed one defense; reveal the identity of the person trying to frame Elizabeth. Someone who knew her and the man sitting across from me. I needed to make lists.

"You've a good memory," I said over coffee.

Marsh sipped. "I'll remember you owe me. I've saved you some legwork and I will expect a return."

"If I can. Don't mention that Elizabeth has me working the streets for her and I'll owe you double. At least until the cops and D.A. make a move on her."

"That's a big favor, Clay. I make my living on timeliness and knowledge no one else has."

"I don't see any out-of-town papers picking up on her, do you?"

"My fame spreads far. But they'd have to make some calls or even send a liner here. In these 'keep the costs down' days, they'd just as soon buy my feed from the Herald."

I saw Cassie come in for her shift. Jonas wouldn't be far behind for his. "I'll give you one tip."

Marsh put down his cup and took out a notebook. "What's the tip?"

"Concentrate on Mendez's side of the story. I'm betting that's where the police are." Dennis' first step had been to scout Mendez's locale. Maybe the police didn't swallow the Elizabeth Rudge connection either.

"Mendez used to be easy to access, not so much since his attack. I've heard rumors he may relocate to another state. I think he's afraid the shooting was more than a warning."

"What do you think?"

"Outside my expertise," said Marsh.

"I'm going to observe him this weekend at one of his charity auctions."

"I'll see you there. We'll tag team him."

"I want to limit my interaction as strictly social this time. Get a feel for what the guy's like."

Marsh laughed. "You'll learn what he wants you to learn. The many faces of Oscar Mendez are presented one at a time." Marsh stood. "Thanks for lunch."

"You're welcome. And I still owe you. Just try to keep my details private for now."

Jonas came in as I exited. "Leaving so soon?"

"Yeah, I had an early lunch with Colin Marsh, ace reporter and the man who got the tip on Elizabeth Rudge."

Jonas held up a Herald in his fist. "I read. Will you be tomorrow's feature?"

"I hope not. If I am, my days of working for Farina-Black are done."

"Where you off to?"

"My place and then the hospital," I said. "I want to check on the guy who tried to punt me off the road."

Chapter 7

I phoned Ynez from my condo and left a message about a change in venue for Saturday's soiree. "Dress formal. Like a faculty function. Let me know if you're game. It should be entertaining and Pops says we don't have to buy anything."

Dennis Levi had left a message for me to meet him at the courthouse station later in the afternoon.

I drove to the hospital and accessed the room number through the names the accident investigator had supplied. Buddy Tkachuk was in ICU. The nurse read me the summary. "Fourteen fractures, hand lacerations, internal bleeding," she glanced up to make eye contact, "now stopped, organ failure on three fronts."

"A day in the life of Evel Knievel," I said.

Her look told me what she knew about Evel would fill the end of a cotton swab.

I changed gears. "Can he talk?"

"He's on a morphine drip. He can talk but not coherently. Are you a relative?"

"No."

Her eyes narrowed. "Close friend?"

"No. I have to be honest with you, I was right behind them when he and his driver crashed. It shook me up. I slowed down because I knew the road. I tried to signal the danger but they were onto the frost and down in a heartbeat. I'd like to talk to the guy and see what I can do."

She thought for a moment. "All right. Five minutes and I'm off shift. I'll escort you out then."

She led me through a door festooned with red and yellow warning stickers. If I looked closely, I'm sure I could find one elaborating the danger of sitting in a chair with less than six legs. We turned left and entered a two-bed room with only one occupant. She pulled the curtain surround to admit me.

Buddy Tkachuk was tubed, wired, bandaged and strapped. He had more electronics surrounding him than a Best Buy store. His face was uninjured but his skin was waxy. The cheeks were drawn in and with his grey-peppered beard, he looked double my age.

"How old is he?"

"Thirty-one," said the nurse.

"He looks sixty."

I leaned close to his ear. "Buddy, are you with us man?"

I watched his eyelids flutter. Doped but not completely out of it.

"I saw the crash," I said. "You went down hard."

"S...skid. Flip. Wh...where's Steve?" He coughed and I stepped back from the spume. I didn't come to the hospital to get sick.

"Steve's around," I lied. "How come you tried to wreck that other bike?" No sense in telling him it was me. Not yet.

"S...Steve hired me. Easy jo...job."

The nurse tugged my arm. "You have to leave."

"Did you hear him?"

"Hear what?" She was busy making checkmarks on the clipboard in her hand.

"I had the image of Buddy trying to kick my bike as they went past. Before the skid. He just confirmed Steve hired him to do it."

She shook her head as we walked past the nurse's station and she dropped her clipboard. "I'm sorry, I didn't hear it."

"I may return with a sheriff and question Buddy again before a witness. What time is your next shift?" I ready her name tag. "Mrs. Figuaredo." I'd also spotted the wedding band.

"*Betsy*. I start at four a.m."

"I'm usually weeding my garden then. I'll let you get a few hours under your belt before I come back." I had to push my pace to keep up with her. "Has anyone else visited him? Who's paying for his care?"

"He had one visitor at nine. Steve. Spent less time than you did with him. He asked directions to the billing administrator's office when he left so I assume he took care of the coverage."

"Thanks. Where is billing?" ICU wouldn't be cheap. Buddy didn't look like a guy with extensive medical insurance. This was costing someone big dollars. I followed her directions and ran into a brick wall. Not a real brick wall but an administrative one. Patient coverage information was more sacred than the medical diagnosis. I tried, failed and left before hospital security volunteered to help me find the exit. I didn't want to be banned before my next visit, dragging Dennis with me.

Chapter 8

It was a gorgeous afternoon and I was tempted to fire up the Goldstar and play hooky but I had work to do. I went home and set up my workspace on the balcony overlooking Monterey Bay. I stuffed in a pair of cycle earplugs to drown out the street traffic and began making notes.

I listed the tasks before me in random order. Timing would come later. Mendez's class-action suitors; investors who weren't in the lawsuits but lost money and wished to remain anonymous; those who knew the Rudges and Mendez; and something to appease Marsh so he didn't publicize Farina-Black. I needed to call the Securities Commission. On second thought, that might be more productive from someone in Pops' firm. Maybe Audrey Ellis or Milt Canyon had a contact.

The time passed and I had a good idea of my future activities between now and Saturday's auction. I checked my watch and realized my next appointment was with Dennis. Twenty minutes ago.

I phoned the station to say I was on my way.

The County Sheriff's office resided within the Monterey Courthouse. Dennis waved me into the bullpen when I arrived, a peace-offering latte in my hand.

"You're not joining me, Clay?" He peeled the lid free and blew before a sip.

"Only had time to get one made up. Sorry about the delay. I was trying to put my thoughts together on the Mendez-Rudge deal. She's Pops' client and now mine."

"Interesting. I've already had a call from her lawyer."

I sat. "General inquiry or threat?"

"I'd say both. No discernable threat but an underlying tone that I, we, should go easy until we had a viable case against her."

Roger Schopff had planted his seed, now it was my turn. "I doubt you will. Five years between shootings, if it was her gunning Mendez, is a long time to tie together an emotional similarity. Her attack on Gordon Rudge was alcohol-fuelled emotion. She's be dry since her arrest in that case. Elizabeth was paroled early for displaying emotional stability, among other rationale. I'd say let her alone and use the opportunity to find the real shooter."

Dennis set the drink on his desk. He dragged a four-inch-high stack in front of him. "Don't you think we've been trying. Despite what you, the press and the public may think, we haven't let the Mendez case drop; we just have nothing further to go on."

"Not even one major suspect?"

"Just the opposite. Too many. And the only eyewitness, the victim, didn't get a good enough look to help."

I gestured toward the pile. "May I?"

He pushed it forward. "Be my guest."

I quit counting names after thirty. It was ground I'd need to cover. "Can I make a list of the names and highlights? I'm going to approach Elizabeth's defense, if it comes to that, from Mendez's side as well as hers. Maybe there's a commonality you haven't dug up that I might. On the financial side."

"Excuse me, I have to make some calls." Dennis picked up his phone and ignored me as I pulled out my notebook. He made four calls and took two restroom breaks while I abbreviated the data for each name. Twenty-eight men and thirteen women. I noted statements from them, mostly 'not sorry for him', 'relieved he isn't dead, maybe we'll recoup some funds' and 'it wasn't me'. I abbreviated the alibis, few ironclad but worth checking at some point, most people wouldn't have one that early in the day. I listed the stated losses; I dig into those, see who recovered and whose lifestyle was severely impacted.

I straightened the pile and put away my notebook as Dennis settled into his chair. "Who else have you spoken with besides your dad, Rudge and her lawyer?"

"Colin Marsh." No sense hiding it since Cassie had seen Marsh and I together.

Dennis sat up. He didn't know. His wife hadn't told him. Yet. "I don't want any of the information you copied showing up in the media. It does and I'll nut you."

"Don't worry. I owe him but none of this is for his eyes. Or anyone's for that matter. I may ask Elizabeth if she knows any of them?"

"I'd rather you didn't. She'd tell Schopff and he'd exploit it."

"Come on, Dennis. If he could use anything, then it'd mean he has cause."

"Not necessarily. He could undermine evidence by bringing into question irrelevant data." He reached out his hand. "Otherwise, I'll ask you for that notebook."

I held it tighter. Not a hill I wanted to die upon. "Okay. You have a deal. I won't reveal these. I will ask her for names of people she knew as fellow investors. I get hits, I'll pass them on to you." Eventually.

"Fair enough."

"I've another favor to ask."

"Wasn't this sufficient for a day's work?"

"Unrelated. Have you had a chance to research the two bikers from the accident? Buddy Tkachuk and Steve Rokon."

"No time yet. You in a hurry?"

"The passenger, Buddy, is in tough, medical-wise." I relayed Buddy's words in the hospital. "I'd like you to accompany me on my next visit to witness his statement."

"How doped is he?"

"Extremely."

"Statement's an inch above worthless."

"I know. But having someone else hear it, especially an officer of the law would make me feel better."

"Okay. When?"

"Tomorrow morning. I'll call and meet you there."

"Where should I start with these guys?"

"See if Steve is still in town. Otherwise, backtrack to San Luis Obispo. I've a hunch they're revenge hires for a job I completed down there for Pops. Divorce property settlement. Evil dentist."

"Yeah, we get a lot of those." Dennis could hold a straight face forever.

It took a few moments before I realized he was joking. "Ha, ha. This particular one was hiding profits in half a dozen places. Not only from his wife but the IRS. He never hit his wife but he didn't take mistress break-ups peacefully."

Dennis rose to his feet. My time here was done.

"I'll see you tomorrow, Clay."

I tapped my pocket. "Thanks for the info. When we get to the bottom of this, I'll ensure you get all the credit due."

"For doing my job?"

"For proving your job has worth. Not a universal opinion these days."

Chapter 9

I crashed early and hard. Gull screeches woke me at dawn. I closed my windows and crawled back to bed until almost eight o'clock. Pops would have been mowing the lawn by now outside my window if I still lived at home. By the way, he still mowed his own grass.

Ingrained habits battled my attempt to remain horizontal. I admitted defeat, arose and opened the blinds. Half a dozen sails dotted the bay. Not everyone had to work. The sky was cloudless and I wished I could trade a day scoping names and stories for a ride up to Half Moon Bay and back on the bike. But the Clay Farina Confidential Investigations Corporation does not slack during times of employment. Pops would retire in the next few years and my 'in' with my Farina-Black might migrate from the investment business to the golf course. I couldn't picture myself golfing to recruit clients. And I certainly didn't golf to relax. I rode.

I brewed coffee and began writing the names from Dennis' file onto individual file cards. Behind the times, computerwise? Absolutely. Luddite? No. The very act of writing the details by hand helps to file them in my brain. Pinning them onto my cork wall gave them peripheral life. Sometimes a subconscious view triggered connections which weren't obvious on a monitor.

My business phone rang on the second cup and halfway through the list.

"Clay Farina speaking."

A female voice I didn't recognize addressed me. "Mr. Farina? Good. This is Jolene Rudge."

I racked memory. Elizabeth's daughter or Gordon's second wife? "Yes, how can I help?"

"I'd like to speak with you. Today if possible. Wednesday is my errand day and I'm in Monterey now. I can come by your office. I have the address from your card."

The daughter. She'd got the card from Elizabeth. I had to grab Dennis and take him to the hospital to see Buddy. "Does eleven work for you?" Give me time to finish the first run through and clean up.

"I'll see you then." She hung up.

"You're welcome," I said to the ceiling.

I phoned Dennis and he agreed to meet in the ICU. I drew a curtain across the cork board and stowed the unpinned cards in a drawer.

The Wednesday edition of the County Herald was on time. I bought a copy and a British classic motorcycle mag from my news dealer. Monday's breaking news was pushed to page two by 'Tragic Death At Sea', the whale non-expose.

I flipped past the dead cetacean story. I was interested in the living this morning. Colin Marsh's follow-up column to Monday's coverage focused away from Elizabeth Rudge and Mendez. This was social commentary. Marsh speculating on the harm suffered by extended family during the dissolution of a marriage. Colin didn't name names but anyone familiar with the story wouldn't have to try hard.

The abusive ex-husband as a victim. A stretch for me but Colin scored a few solids with the insight that the couple's immediate circle could have done more to alleviate the abuse.

Children got a few column inches as well. Their victimization would've begun as pre-school witnesses, thinking the abnormality was normal. It answered the question he'd raised in the previous paragraph.

Friends and social circle wrapped up the portrait of a violently dysfunctional family. The teaser for the next installment promised an evaluation of the legal system's record on domestic violence and justice.

It was a well-crafted piece and sure to sell a few more papers on Friday for part three.

Nurse Betsy ushered Dennis and me behind Buddy's curtain. The machines were still in full swing but Buddy's eyes were closed.

"Buddy, it's me, the guy you tried to crash. Remember we spoke yesterday?"

"I fell." His eyes flickered open.

"Yeah. You lost your balance trying to kick me from my bike. Steve lost control on the frost and you crashed."

"St...Steve? He's back?" Buddy's eyes swiveled back and forth.

"You're not Steve."

"No. I'm the other rider. You admitted yesterday you deliberately tried to crash me. Can you repeat what you said?"

"Steve cr...crashed. I broke m...my arm, I think. Or leg."

"Look at me, Buddy." I moved my head closer, eye to eye. "Why did you try to wreck me?"

"No." Buddy closed his eyes and clammed up.

"Well, shit," I grumbled.

Dennis identified himself and asked questions but Buddy had said all he was going to today. After ten minutes, Dennis straightened up and looked at me. "Well, shit."

"Thanks for trying, Dennis. Guess I'll have to talk to Steve, if and when I get a chance." I looked at my watch. "Gotta fly, my client's daughter is due at my office in fifteen minutes."

"Don't break any speed laws on your way," he said.

MY 'OFFICE' WAS DESIGNED originally as a guest room or study right beside the front entry. It had a secure passage door installed to separate it from my living quarters.

While I waited for Jolene Rudge, I retrieved the cards, memorizing names. I'd have to ask Jonas about the daughter. I added her to the card stack. I searched my memory to the original Rudge case. There was a brother. I added another card for the sibling.

Precisely at eleven, the bell rang and I opened up for Jolene Rudge. She was a hearty-looking outdoor type in a plaid shirt, denim skirt and matching blazer. The cowboy hat in her hand was well broken in and she wore it constantly if the forehead tan line didn't lie.

"Clay Farina, nice to meet you." I held out my hand and got a healthy, callused grip.

"Mr. Farina." She entered my office and took a seat before I could offer it. Jolene crossed her legs, displaying turquoise riding boots and set the hat on her knee.

"Correct me if I'm wrong but you're Elizabeth's daughter, right?" The slightly square jaw was the main resemblance.

"Elizabeth *and* Gordon's daughter."

Not entirely mommy's girl, I realized. "Naturally. I've only met your mother. Yesterday."

"She told me. Mr. Farina, I don't see a lot of my mother these days. My small ranch keeps me busy and away from her circle."

Circle? My impression was Elizabeth was a recluse, not necessarily by choice. Good to know she'd retained or developed some friendships.

"Where do you live, Ms. Rudge?"

"Salinas Valley. I run a riding school."

Better to own one than pay for your offspring to attend one. "I appreciate you saving me a trip out there, though I'd like to see it, if I get the chance. Are you here on her behalf, your father's or your own?"

Jolene fussed with her hat, uncrossed her legs, then crossed them the other way. "All, I guess. I can't control what the newspapers print." She dropped her copy of Colin Marsh's article on my desk.

"Ah," I said. Brilliant. Start treading water with more vigor. "I've seen that. I'm sorry your family's notoriety can't be forgotten."

She gave me a steely look. If I was a horse, I'd have lowered my head.

"I can't control rumors or what the police investigate. I won't pretend I can control you either, Mr. Farina. This latest allegation is unwarranted but it's out there. My mother has just begun to re-emerge from social exile. That's how long it takes in this community. But the publicity will hurt dad as well. He hasn't had it easy, having his infidelities dragged through the public eye. This latest rumor will reveal his sins once again. How many times does he have to pay?"

"I appreciate your concern. Too often we forget there's more than one side."

"There is. Dad was a prick to my mother. And she to him. They both fed on the other's pain, often publicly."

"Tough on you. Your brother as well?" I tested my memory. Colin's article had been generic on the family, not specific.

"Lawrence moved to Denver after the trial. He would reiterate my concerns for dad."

Now I had a name for the brother's card. And a location. Not within easy reach except by phone. "I'd planned to talk to your dad at some point."

"I'd rather you didn't."

"I understand your desire to protect him but the shorter I can make this process, the better for him. It's out there, Ms. Rudge. I'm not engaged to hurt your dad. I'm hired to ensure this Mendez link goes away. To expedite, I need to talk to as many relevant people as I can in a short period. Give the media and the police another line of inquiry, one which leads them away from family Rudge."

"I'd hoped I could convince you otherwise. Obviously, you represent mother first." She looked disheartened. The anger from before had drained from her.

I wanted to push but chose a conciliatory tone instead. "How about this? You arrange for me to meet your dad and in your presence. If I cross a line, you shut me down."

"I can suggest it to him." She fished a phone from a leather-tooled purse.

"Do you want privacy?" I leaned forward to stand.

She shook her head. The phone was ringing. "Hi dad, it's me. No, I'm in Pacific Grove. Yeah, I talked to her yesterday. You read it? How fucked up is that? I know. Listen, I'm meeting the guy Farina-Black hired to help clear her name. Don't say that. Anyway, he'd like to talk with you and I'm thinking we can drop in today. I can circle through Santa Cruz and drive home from there. I think it would be helpful for him to meet you. Get this put away and get on with our respective lives. No, it doesn't end." She looked at me. "You okay with this afternoon?"

I nodded. I had to start somewhere. Santa Cruz would be a nice ride. I'd get my two-wheeled Zen today while working.

"Okay dad, see you after lunch. I've a few more errands here. 'Bye."

"I can text you his slip." Her finger was poised over her phone.

"You'd better write it down. He's in the marina?" Worse ways to fall from society's grace, I thought. Depending on the size of his boat.

"Yeah, I'll meet you there."

Jolene Rudge stood and for the first time I noticed she was a good three inches taller than me. But she was in boots and I was in sandals.

She left and I noted another thing. The Salinas Valley was a back door to Mendez's. Ranchers carried guns too. Not necessarily pistols, but why stop at having a few varmint rifles handy. Hell, the ammunition store probably threw in a pocket .22 just for being a good customer.

I ARRIVED IN SANTA Cruz early. The bike made supreme time. I parked near the boardwalk and took lunch out onto the beach, using my helmet for a seat. Monterey Bay's north end was quiet; a few surfers tried to coax rides from tiny waves. They were following a passion and even the shortest motorcycle or wave ride was better than sitting and waiting for arteries to harden and joints to stiffen all on their own.

I finished the meal and made my way to the protected marina. Gordon Rudge's yacht was barely that, a thirty-five-footer by my estimate. Moorage for it wouldn't be cheap despite its modest length. No masts, no sails, just diesel power to cruise when and where he wanted. A dockhand scrubbed the varnished hardwood and fiberglass hull. I walked the length of the vessel to read the name. "The Lucky Roll" script was flanked by two dice, each showing up five. A bit cheeky, I thought but good for Gordon, taking the trauma in stride.

Jolene appeared on the gangplank. "Come on up, dad's waiting."

A slim, short woman with a deep tan, wearing white slacks and a yellow blouse shoved past Jolene. She could've been anywhere between twenty-five and forty-five years old. It was hard to tell behind the enormous sunglasses. I looked below the shades. Her arms were smooth-skinned enough to re-peg the upper age-limit in the 30's. She tossed a County Herald into the water. "Tell your mother I said 'hi' and I hope she did it." She strode past me without a glance. I was outside her ken.

"I'm one of the untouchables," I said to her retreating back. "I mean as in Elliot Ness, not caste-conscious India." I stepped onto the deck. "Let me guess, your step-mother."

"Step-bitch, actually. Tiffany doesn't have a mother gene." Jolene turned and led me inside.

Six steps down and we entered a floating log cabin. I mean, wood inlaid with more wood. Gordon Rudge was a stocky man, no obvious flab around the middle, my height, with black hair combed straight back. His grip was even stronger than his daughter's and they shared similar eyes. Intense.

I sat in the offered chair and sank three inches into ocean-going comfort. "I appreciate you seeing me, Mr. Rudge. How much has Jolene told you?"

"My ex-wife's been linked to Oscar Mendez's shooting. I read it in Monday's paper. Today's column upset Tiffany more than me." He shrugged. "I've had worse experiences."

His voice rasped in contrast to his physical heartiness. Not a terminally sick voice but a weary one. Five slugs would do that to a person. I never wanted to find out first-hand.

"Perhaps you could more fully explain your role, Mr. Farina."

"Please call me Clay. I contract for my father's wealth management firm, Farina-Black. Elizabeth is a client and the news articles have placed her under suspicion. My father likes to take care of his clients. I'm looking to give the police a reason to look elsewhere for Mendez's attacker."

"What if she did it?"

"Dad." Jolene's voice was firm and loud.

Gordon's question was to the point. I wouldn't fool this guy. "Then we find another defense option. Reasonable doubt, emotional trauma, and one or two more alternatives." I looked at Jolene, then him. "Do you think she could have?"

He thought for a minute. "Honestly, no. she'd have to be drunk, really angry and Mendez would have to be cheating on her."

Jolene twitched and squirmed but remained silent.

I said, "You're a candid man, Mr. Rudge."

"I'm aware of my shortcomings. I did not treat my wife well, Clay." He glanced at Jolene. "I am amazed my daughter still speaks to me, let alone seems to like me."

"Dad, the misery cut two ways. Mom wasn't perfect either."

I gave the family reconciliation a moment. I studied the cabin again. The mirrored wall behind Gordon held a small bar. I counted two bottles of hard liquor, both three-quarters full. I guessed his hard-drinking days were over. I asked, "Can you think of anyone who would enjoy Elizabeth being subjected yet again to criminal scrutiny?" My thoughts drifted to the second partner, Tiffany Rudge.

"No. Not anyone who'd go to such lengths to actually try to frame her. Maybe Mendez himself, from what I read and hear, the police have no leads and aren't attempting to get any."

"Do you know him?"

"I knew him. I haven't spoken or dealt with Mendez for years. He swindled many of us smart enough to know better. Greed is a nasty habit, Clay. I suggest you keep your money in a bank. Or a sock."

My cash went for mortgage payments, food and gas. "Not a problem."

"I should've picked a firm like your father's. Well-guided wealth management, not rolling the dice. I lost half of what I had in the divorce, and another half of what I had left to Mendez."

"Are you involved in any of the suits against him?"

"Yeah, for all the good it will do. It'll take years. In the meantime, he'll still be living on his estate and I'll be living on a fucking boat." Rudge stood and looked out a window. "I like living on a boat but I'd like to wake up once in a while on sold ground."

"You can always stay with me, dad," said Jolene.

Rudge laughed. "You and Tiffany under the same roof overnight? One of the three of us would be dead by morning." He looked back at me. "I'm not confessing anything. The ladies do not play well together."

It made me wonder what Tiffany had that prompted him to settle down. Were his philandering days done? She looked like she could pull a trigger if sufficiently motivated.

Rudge returned to his outside view and Jolene stood up. I took the signal and rose. I had another question but it could wait. And I could get the answer from Dennis if needed. "Thanks for your time, Mr. Rudge." I left a business card on the table. "If you think of anything or anyone else which might be relevant, please call me. Or forward a message through Jolene."

"Good luck, Clay. You will have a challenge finding an alternative for Mendez's attacker."

"Why's that?"

"Guys like Mendez exist on a different plane from the rest of us mortals. He is a superhero, invulnerable to everyday nits and minutia. And more importantly, he is invulnerable to remorse, self-doubt or guilt."

"The absence of conscience helps the Teflon persona," I said.

"Nothing sticks," Gordon agreed.

Except two bullets.

Outside, on the pier, Jolene and I stood, watching the scrubber continue his way down Lucky Five.

"Do you think Tiffany would rat out her predecessor?"

"If she could harm my mother, I think she would jump at the chance. This seems beyond her mental capacity. I don't see her as a methodical planner. She's like my dad, lives on impulse."

"A few days at sea can make a person slow down and think, though."

"I suppose it could," she agreed.

I shook Jolene's hand. "Thanks for this. I hope I don't have to bother him again. If I do, I'll go through you, okay?"

"Okay."

The scrubber had finished and was cleaning his equipment at a water station. "You and your dad share a passion for money pits."

"How so?"

"Yachts are holes in the water you pour money into. Stables pour money into the ground."

She patted my helmet. "And vintage British motorcycles?"

"Hole in the garage. Point taken." I hated when someone pierced my illusions of self. Or should it be delusions of self?

Chapter 10

I laid out the cards in my Farina-Black office. While waiting for Pops to be free, I organized name cards into Rudge circles and Mendez circles, tagging the overlaps. Elizabeth and Gordon Rudge would have built separate cliques since the trial, divorce and incarceration, but their children were strong common threads.

Dennis' list concentrated on the Mendez side, obviously, so it took up most of the work table.

The phone rang. "Yes?"

"You wanted me to call." It was Pops.

"Did you have a chance to make up the client list of Mendez investors?"

"It's on its way."

I had another thought. "Say Pops, what about a list of Farina-Black employees who might have bitten?" I held the phone away from my ear until his rant abated. "I know it's a long shot but there are a few institutions named as claimants in the lawsuits, I thought someone here might've taken a flyer with their own money. Not unethical, I'd say. I don't want to get anyone fired; I want to get Elizabeth Rudge cleared."

"I did my own digging on that when Mendez's first lawsuit was announced," he answered, an edge still in his voice. "As far as I determined, there were none. I don't control what everyone here does off our time but I expect their best judgement."

"Understood. Thanks."

I put aside the sense that I was covering old ground with Mendez. The police would've started with his inner circle and moved out as standard procedure. They hadn't succeeded and the most likely scenario featured a disgruntled investor. The planning and execution indicated murder was not the motive. Revenge and scaring the crap out of Mendez was the objective. I ranked the suspects by loss, by location, by opportunity, hell I would've done it by weight if I had the information. Nothing leapt out. Not yet.

There was a knock on my door and Milt Canyon entered. "Your dad asked me to prep this."

I stood and moved to block him entering further into my sanctum. The cards were my clues, not for anyone else's eyes. Not yet.

He handed me a list of names. And addresses. Farina-Black clients who'd admitted their folly with Mendez.

"Thanks."

Milt kept a hold on the sheets. "I view this as a breach of trust with our clients. They're embarrassed enough by their association with Mendez. Make certain you use it appropriately and if you have to talk with any of them, distance yourself from Farina-Black."

"That could be difficult, given my name but I know what you mean. It's delicate but they have 'fessed up. Let me go through the names for cross-referencing to the people I already know about and I'll return the list before I leave the office. You'll be around for a couple more hours?" It was 3:30.

"I'll be here until you're done."

"Thanks, Milt. What about a list of other firms who promoted Mendez?"

"I can come up with a few names."

"Great I closed the door behind him. I was pissed at Pops for handing this off to Milt. Or anyone. The fewer people who knew my investigation details, the better. It was too late now, and I had asked Pops to expedite the matter. It was on me.

I copied the names only, in case any surfaced from another source. I could always retrieve Milt's master list for addresses if needed. I marked the ones already on the police list and added the new ones to the pile on Mendez's side.

At 5:00, I arched my back and gathered the cards together. I needed to change focus. I dropped Milt's breach of trust off to him, thanking and assuring him once again, and stepped outside into a lovely autumn evening. A police cruiser pulled up alongside me.

"Dennis," I greeted. "You were my next call. Any luck finding Steve Rokon?"

"Yeah. Hop in."

I wanted to walk to clear my head but who'd turn down a free ride in a cop car redolent with sweat, coffee and disinfectant?

Dennis pulled into traffic and we cruised toward Pacific Grove. "Well?" I asked. "Why the limo service? Did you find Rokon or not?"

Dennis shook his head. "He found us."

"How fortuitous."

"Not for you." He stopped for a traffic light. "He says you crashed them. Wants to press charges." Instead of heading west where I thought we were going, Dennis swung left. Towards the courthouse which served as their headquarters. "We'll need a formal statement."

"Deputy Reiger has it."

"I hope your memory is consistent."

The unknown master mind couldn't take me out by accident, so now whoever hired Steve and Buddy was trying to take me out legally. "Do I need to call Roger Schopff?" I wanted to speak with Roger on an Elizabeth-related matter anyway.

"It's up to you. You'd be interrupting his supper. Why don't you wait? Read the complaint first?"

ROKON'S STATEMENT READ like fiction. "It's ludicrous," I said. "He claims we were racing for over ten miles and I continually blocked him and finally I got so mad I clipped them and they went down." I threw the paper across the desk. "Did you see their bike? It's got twice the horsepower of my beezer, stickier tires and the throttle response is lightning quick. If we were racing for ten miles, with enough straightaways to blow by me anytime he chose, he must've stayed in second gear."

"Hey, I didn't say I believed it. I have to observe form. Make your statement."

I dictated what I'd told Reiger on Monday, confident I'd not altered any details. "Why has Rokon taken until now to fabricate a new story?"

"A shrewd lawyer would ask why you didn't press charges first."

"That's easy. I didn't crash." And I wasn't certain beyond any reasonable doubt.

"But they tried, according to you. They crashed accidentally. Luck on your side that you didn't?"

"I knew the road and what the hell I was doing."

Dennis had me sign my statement. "It will be filed and investigated when we have time. For the moment it's his word against yours. I'll press him once I've more physical evidence."

"Damn, I wish Buddy had been lucid this morning. It would have saved you time and paperwork."

Dennis witnessed the statement and set it aside. "I doubt it'll go anywhere, given what you just said. My guess is Rokon's trying to inconvenience you since their first plan didn't work. Watch your back."

"Who are these guys?"

Dennis shook his head. "Citizens. Just two buddies out for cruise."

I shook my head. "No, they weren't. Dig deeper if you can. They were tailing me until an opportunity arose to take me out. I'm not saying they tried to kill me, I'm saying they were trying to send a message. The dentist case in San Luis Obispo is the most likely source but I can't drop Elizabeth Rudge's investigation to backtrack what should be a closed affair."

Dennis opened another file. Inside was one small note on pink form paper. A phone message. "We had a call about you from a Securities Exchange Commission case manager. Wanted to know what we had on you." He flipped me the note. A name and title.

"Percy Oaks, blah blah blah." I passed it back. "Percy?"

"What the man said."

"What did you tell him?"

"You were in good standing with us. An occasional ally, in fact."

"Thanks. Did he say why he needed to know?" Had the dentist ratted on me? More inconvenience?

"No. I offered him your phone number but he said he already had it."

"Anything else? I'm tired and hungry."

"Go home."

"Nope. I'm walking to the Grill and drown my inconveniences in beer and crab."

"If I wasn't on duty, I'd join you."

"Next time. Do you ever feel odd having Cassie serve you?"

"Yup. That's why she works the day shift, so I can serve her at home. When I'm home."

I envied them both. They had a solid marriage despite his being in a profession known for chewing up relationships. My investigator career was less stressful, less traumatic but then I had no relationship to sabotage.

Careful, I thought. You need to purge those thoughts before Saturday evening. Ynez doesn't deserve an emotional avalanche on a first date. Or second. Or ever. Geez, I was planning too far ahead already. Beer me.

Chapter 11

The phone deserved to be shot. At least the ringtone. Hungover or not, the clanging should be replaced by a soothing female voice. Something like, "Wake up, precious." Or "I've made you breakfast, dear." Or "My husband's home."

I rolled to my feet and answered it, pulling on socks, just in case.

"Hello." Knuckle eyes and search for water.

"Mr. Farina?"

"One of them." Don't give me your money, my socks are full of feet.

"*Clay* Farina?"

"You got the right one. Who am I speaking too?" Tongue working again despite the extra coat of mung.

"My name is Percy Oaks with the California Securities Commission."

"Right, Dennis Levi told me you'd contacted him. How can I help you, Mr. Oaks?" There was no way I'm calling this guy Percy and his rather dour tone suggested he wouldn't like it either.

"It's a matter we should discuss in person. Are you free this morning?"

"Give me half an hour." If he had relevant information to my case, better to see him soon and eliminate potential dead ends. "My home office?"

"I'll be there."

He hung up before he had a chance to thank me. Shower, coffee and toast. And try not to have crumbs on my face when Mr. Oaks arrived.

He was right on time, probably phoned from the street and set his stopwatch. Oaks didn't look like an accountant. He was tall, medium build, didn't wear glasses but did wear a suit. His light brown hair was shaved high on the sides. Top moussed to spikes. The soap opera look extended to a carefully trimmed six-day length beard stubble. Neither did he carry a briefcase. I thought they all had briefcases. I guess my interview didn't rank. It was all in his head.

"Percy Oaks," he repeated in person.

He passed an impressive shiny black business card with silver print. I studied it. It said Percy Oaks right enough.

"Have a seat, Mr. Oaks."

He brushed the guest chair and sat.

"Coffee?"

"No, thank you." He examined my headquarters in a glance.

I flipped his card in my hand while I waited for him to start. If this was going on Farina-Black's billing, I should have paper and pen ready. I put down his card and arranged a notepad. I sipped coffee, then wrote his name on the top of the first page. I smiled. Oaks didn't.

"You're investigating Oscar Mendez." It wasn't a question.

"Not yet, should I?"

"Don't be literal, Mr. Farina. I know you've been making inquiries."

"Following up leads related to a client, not Mendez. His involvement is critical. I've been seeking information about his shooting eight months ago and his business life seems to dovetail in."

"Your dovetail could jeopardize the Commission's investigation."

"How long have you been pursuing this investigation?"

"That's classified."

"Well, it must be recent or you wouldn't be bothering me. From what I hear, Mendez has been skirting California Securities law for years. And you're investigating now to cover your own asses in light of numerous civil suits, launched when the Commission failed to take action against a slew of complaints dating back, oh, let me guess, five years? Ten?" Oaks didn't ruffle.

"Mr. Mendez's investment subscriptions did not violate the letter of the law."

"Letter? Tell that to the people he bankrupted." I was losing patience. Not a good thing if I wanted to get any information from this guy. "Look, I appreciate you have limited manpower, limited resources and limited deterrent options. Can I help?"

"You can help by backing off Mendez. We'll get him. When we do, it'll be lock solid and he won't be doing business in California or any other state."

I pulled Monday's newspaper from a drawer and slid it to him. "I have a client accused of his shooting. I have a duty to her and anyone who's watching to prove she didn't do it. Attempted murder trumps financial malfeasance, doesn't it?"

"The Commission is only interested in the economic crime." He slid the paper back. "Farina-Black is your client. Elizabeth Rudge is theirs. You are separated from her by a degree."

"Uh uh," I said. "In this matter, I am Farina-Black. There is no degree of separation."

"My advice is to preserve Farina-Black's standing with my agency."

Oaks stood. I stood.

"Go easy, Mr. Farina."

I didn't like his advice but I didn't know how much influence he swung. "Easy this case is not, Mr. Oaks. You could make it easier by sharing information. In all your digging, you must have come across at least one investor who was beyond normal anger. One who you judged could be violent. I'd think in the basis of public safety, you'd at least share that with the police, if not me."

"Good day, Mr. Farina."

Oaks didn't act like he'd share his shoe size. I didn't like his threat against Pops and I'm certain Pops wouldn't either. Maybe he'd know someone up the Commission's tree who could pass a few names onto the police.

Oaks' visit didn't turn out to be the boost I wanted to begin my day. Very well, I'd review my own lists and start scouting. See who'd maintained the rich and famous lifestyle and who'd come down in the world. Then I'd talk to Jonas.

Chapter 12

17 Mile Drive, like the early stages of most investigations, lay shrouded in fog. I could glimpse and hear breakers crashing against the shore along Pebble Beach. Halfway to the southern limit, the sky cleared enough for my main objective, a visual scan of properties owned by some Mendez investors. I wasn't sure what I was hunting for but the drive was a chance to purge Percy Oaks' superior attitude and unjustified intimidation.

My bug convertible was out of place by its advanced age and non-SUV status amongst the blacked-out nanny-mobiles ferrying their charges to and from private school.

The first hit on my list of potential Mendez sufferers gleamed with brass gates set into single pillars of stone, marble? Someone was still being paid to polish the alloy. I slowed to get a view through the bars. The mansion appeared pristine from two hundred feet. I made an 'X' and drove on.

Four more estates upheld their station in life appropriate to the community and I turned around to eyeball the few I'd missed in the fog. The second last address was no longer pristine. The grounds were landscaped but not this week. Or the week before. Neat but shaggy, I wrote. In another month, it would be overgrown unless the groundskeeper's check cleared.

The final house remained immaculate. I pulled off and sat, staring out at the Pacific. The waves curled and foamed in their inexorable assault against the land. They eroded but they brought sand, shells and kelp by the ton to our shore. Destruction was relative. Money came and went too.

I circled the name of the house owner allowing their frontage to run downhill. A favor from DMV might reveal how many upscale vehicles, if any, were still in the fleet?

One descent out of ten names on my list. Did it relate to Mendez or had the family over-extended due to other factors? What else did I have to rely on besides Farina-Black client and public lawsuit lists?

What about those who weren't involved in the suits or Pops' firm? Why not? Couldn't afford to pay legal fees? Not all of the suits were contingency based. Something this large required a team of lawyers. Specialists in investment fraud. Large fees put that out of small investors' reach. That was one reason. Embarrassment could be another. Even though your friends could be victims too, you might hold on to a superiority complex in public but privately wish for bad things to happen to Mendez. The blow from financial loss could be softened by a lead salute. A flock of geese honked overhead and I stuck my head out my window to watch them maintain their 'V' formation.

Leader at the point. A third possibility occurred to me. An investment advisor. There were a couple in the list who'd sunk clients' money into Mendez's schemes and been willing to publicize their fall and take action on behalf of their clients. What about someone in an investment firm putting their own money in? Or company money? Their publicity wouldn't be welcome. It could cost them reputation and position.

Crap, I'd just made my circle of suspects larger. That wasn't how it was supposed to work. You drew the circle tighter until one remained. I'd need a bus to round them all up. I backed from the lot and headed north.

POPS WAS OUT SO I HEADED for the Bay Grill. Maybe Jonas could shed light on my quandary.

"You're looking unperky, Jonas, disgruntled."

He wore my eyebags from my too early wake up this morning.

"When have I ever been 'gruntled'?"

"I've seen you perky. What dire misfortune brings down my friend? I will vanquish thine enemy as if my own. Wine off?" I chose water regardless. Clue-hunting was thirsty work.

"I apologize for my sour mood. It shall lift. Nothing you can do unless you have the power of Gaia within your righteous soul."

"Not likely. Purge and then we can get to my problem of the hour."

"It's Warren Zevon's fault."

I chuckled. "Isn't everything? Wasn't everything? You can't blame him for anything now."

"I can," said Jonas. "His music lives on after the flesh is gone. They played 'Desperadoes Under the Eaves' this morning and the one line has become my earwig." Jonas sang it, "And if California slides into the ocean."

"Like the mystics in statistics say it will," I finished. "He was just rhyming."

Jonas shook his head. He swirled his wine glass in both hands. "I think he was prescient. His own death came before the *big one*."

"We all know the big one will happen. We hope our deaths transpire before it hits. The price for living in paradise," I said. "Remember, we do live in paradise." I looked around the Grill. "Maybe not in this one spot but walk outside along the bay. I toured 17 Mile Drive this morning and fog or sun, it's beautiful. On our doorstep. And it's a huge frigging doorstep. Nothing between it and Japan except five or six thousand miles of blue water. We'll have a new shoreline. Not everyone's sliding into the ocean, only those who can afford to relocate."

"It's true I don't reside proximal, except during my hours here." Jonas counted fingers. "There is a one in two or maybe two in three chance I will be at home during the splash. And awaken to discover I now reside in beach-front property." He pumped a finger near my chest. "Valuable beach property. I feel I can go on."

"Cheers." I lifted my water. "One dilemma solved. More to ponder."

"You have a dilemma?"

"I do. My investigation is going in reverse. The suspect base keeps growing instead of shrinking through elimination."

"Isn't that a good thing? Makes Elizabeth Rudge one of a hundred potential shooters."

"I'd rather find the genuine one, then her case evaporates rather than muddles. She's vindicated beyond doubt in the law's eyes and, more importantly, the public's."

"I appreciate you want such a solution as best case outcome. Still, start with the inner circle and move out."

"I know. I've been coming at it from both directions, hoping to reach a 'Eureka' moment in the middle. The only inner circle I can penetrate for now is my client's. Elizabeth Rudge, her daughter, her ex-husband and his wife. Let's start with Tiffany. Her resentment toward the first Mrs. Rudge seems intense." I quoted her words by Gordon's yacht.

Jonas sipped. "The second wife blames the first wife's settlement on her and Gordon's throttled-back lifestyle. Tiffany thinks Elizabeth should have been content with venting her anger with bullets and stopped Gordon's bleeding then and there. Divorce quietly in another jurisdiction for a modest sum. Instead, California divorce settlements tend to favor the non-working spouse. Elizabeth could've got more, if he'd had any more."

"Tiffany isn't alone in her resentment. Gordon was angry he had to 'live on a fucking boat' to parrot his words. No land option. He liked having an estate and a boat."

"He entertained a lot on that boat," said Jonas. "Elizabeth didn't care for the nautical life, I'm told."

"It's likely Tiffany spent time aboard before she became his wife. She's tired of the marina life, too." I dug into my sandwich. "It gives either of them reason for revenge but it doesn't restore what they've lost. What about the daughter, Jolene? She's running a riding school. That can't be cheap. Again, why would she fit either crime? Shooting Mendez or framing her own mother?"

"Revenge for the first, no sense for the second. Are they close? Her and mama?"

"I think their relationship hasn't healed from the strain of the shooting trial. She was caught in the middle of a very public scrap. The shooting was a small part, a minor climax to years of abuse, on both sides, continual rancor and trying to drag her and her brother into taking sides. I'm surprised she speaks to either one."

"The brother. Denver?"

"Your memory for detail strikes again. Bang on. Not sure he's a suspect yet. Back to the second Mrs. Rudge. Maybe Tiffany's disappointment in their life boiled over. Mendez was as strong a target as Elizabeth. Think she's smart enough to cook up shooting Mendez? Not to kill, wait for eight months to pass, then point the finger at Elizabeth?"

"I've no idea. I've only encountered Tiffany a few times and that was from a distance. She struck me as an intellectual lightweight but could be an act."

"I need a criminal savant." I slipped the stack of file cards from my pocket and riffled them. "It's hard to eliminate people I haven't met. Names, addresses and a financial sketch aren't enough to eliminate or pursue further."

Jonas spread the cards across the table like a magician's playing card deck. "You're pushing too hard. It's clouding your judgment."

"No choice. Delay won't help Elizabeth's emotional state."

"Are you sure about her fragility? Maybe you should retract your nets and start on the inside in detail. She'd be the first interview since Mendez isn't easily accessible."

It was possible I was trying to protect someone who had the means to protect themselves. "You're right. Good call. I wanted to speak with her prison counsellor first. Get a sense of who she was versus who she is now."

I went over to the bar. "Cassie, can I use the phone?"

"As long as you're not calling the south pole, sure."

She passed me the receiver and I dialled.

"Roger Schopff, please. It's Clay Farina. Roger? Glad I caught you. I have a couple of things I'd like to go over in person, if you have time this afternoon."

"I have a partner meeting at two, how long do you need?"

I checked my watch. Twelve-thirty. "Less than an hour. I can be there in ten minutes."

"Come ahead, Clay."

"Thanks." I handed the phone back to Cassie.

"Why don't you get a cell phone?"

"Heard they're dangerous to the brain cells."

"Keep it in your back pocket."

"Where do you think I keep my brain?"

I picked up the cards. Jonas' index finger was conducting business on his cellphone. "Are you up or down today?"

"I shouldn't have looked," he said.

"At least you didn't sink money into Mendez's rathole." I paused when he didn't make eye contact. "You didn't, right?"

"Of course not. My discretionary funds went into power generation facility upgrades. Looked at your electricity bill lately? In detail?"

"Not in detail. I don't question bargains."

"Surplus of power, surplus of plants. Big tax breaks and investment return rates encourage overbuilding. We're at higher capacity than California can use."

"What about your guaranteed return?"

"Doesn't apply to the private entities burning my money."

"Worth shooting anyone?"

Jonas laughed. "No. Have you ever shot anyone?"

"A cuckoo clock."

"Justified. Where are you rushing?"

"Elizabeth's lawyer." Maybe my lawyer if Mr. Oaks of the black and silver business card became more agitated with me. Or Steve Rokon's claim gained traction.

Chapter 13

Roger Schopff greeted me from behind his massive desk. "What's on your mind, Clay? Any progress on Elizabeth's case?"

"Too much and too little," I said. "My list of potential Mendez shooters grows. Virtually any investor had motive. The police covered most of the ground. I thought with another half a year passing, the more vulnerable dupes would be obvious. Changes in lifestyle."

"It's hard to maintain an economic façade for long if you've a high cash burn-rate. Descending the social register can be a symptom or result."

"Exactly. There are a few possibles and I'll keep digging. I'll ask Dennis Levi if he can give me a cross-referenced list of gun range members. It's something they should have checked before putting the case in the 'hold' pile."

"What about people who might have tried the frame on Elizabeth?"

"The ex-husband or his current wife are both solid candidates as far as motive is concerned. Whether they actually tipped off the police and Colin Marsh, I don't know. It wouldn't take much effort to do it. Just anger, and they both score high on that. I'm still not sure if the tip was about Elizabeth or Mendez. She could be just a convenience. A false trail but the goal is pushing revenge against Mendez."

"Anything else?"

"Three matters. First, there's a group of Mendez associates I haven't scratched. His contractors, cleaners, building maintenance staff and managers. Does he pay on time? Any past or outstanding legal action?"

"I have it checked." More scribbling. "Next?"

"What are the chances of interviewing Elizabeth's prison psychiatrist? He'd be a potential witness for you or the prosecution if this went to trial."

"She'd," he corrected. "Doctor Wendy Tam. I'll put in a call to her office." He scrawled a note.

"I think we both should be present."

"Agreed. What's the last matter?"

"I may need your services." I explained about the accident and the allegation I had been the one attempting to wreck the other bike.

"Mr. Rokon's word against yours, until his passenger regains coherence. You shouldn't count on this Buddy to re-affirm his own guilt." He added their names to his legal pad. "Let me see what our contacts in San Luis Obispo can turn up about them."

"Thanks, I'd run down there myself but I don't have the time to pull back from this investigation."

"I'm pleased with the progress you've made already, Clay. In three days, you've met the immediate family and scoured the crime scene. We'll reconvene Monday after you've seen Mendez in action."

"I hope to add more than mere impressions of the target."

On the street, the mist had turned to mizzle. I jogged to my car and headed to the motor vehicle branch. Dig up what I could on the one residence on 17 Mile Drive looking like the owners were transitioning from caviar to canned tuna.

The title trail for vehicles once registered to Armand Moore was interesting. Tragic, if you saw the disintegration from his point of view. Not from mine; the 'trading down' from Lincoln to second-hand Buick, Hummer to high-mileage Nissan didn't resonate with my existence. My Beetle was a decade older than me. Not that I'm claiming poverty, I like its humility. If I need to go fast, the Goldstar answers any need for speed.

Moore and family were shedding assets. He was on the lawsuit list. Could he hold out until a settlement? What more could he sell before the house had to go?

Another title to check. The property. Liens? Mortgages? How much did he owe? I was stymied at the county title office for real estate. I left a message for Roger, hoping he or someone in his firm had an inside source.

I stopped in front of the County Herald's office. Lights were on through the rain. Time for another research project.

"Hi, Ms. Diaz. Remember me?"

The editor again manned the office solo. "Mr. Farina. Here to subscribe?"

"I buy it from the newsvendor on my street. Regularly. Delivered ones kept getting swiped from our front doors. Tourists, I suspect, wanting a free look at the news."

"Well, at least you're a reader."

"I'd like to dig into your tombs on one of our high-profile citizens. Oscar Mendez."

"Still connected to Colin's story?"

"Yeah, but I'd like to know more about Mendez's family, not his business."

"Have a seat." She booted up a console, typed a password to fast for me to follow, then entered 'Oscar Mendez'. "Have at it."

"Thanks." I unrolled a damp notepad. The search consisted mostly of the shooting story told on different sites, nearly all from one source, the Herald, and reposted on other news pages across the state.

My eyes blurred trying to find original work. At last, I found a two-year-old piece on one of his charity events. The same annual auction I would be attending on Saturday. There was a photograph of Oscar, his wife Cecile and grown son, Oscar Jr., with his wife, unnamed.

Oscar Jr. was slim like his mother, not physically powerful like his father. A good-looking young man, destined for all the good things money could buy. Or if the coin landed tails, tasked with making it on his own. Don't sweat it, Junior, I chose to divert from my father's path and look how I turned out. Following my passion, or avoiding Pops', but still reliant on his love and goodwill to stay in business.

If Oscar Sr. was as savvy as advertised, the family would be provided for no matter what happened to the business. Assets secluded in the Caymans or Switzerland. Maybe even Mexico.

I widened the search, focusing on Junior. Scant but a few morsels popped up. Less-than-stellar university career. In fact, he'd changed schools three times in four years, finally getting a Communications degree, no distinction, from a minor college in Wyoming. You could likely buy it online with enough cash.

Junior's vocation now seemed to be racing cars faster than him at Laguna Seca and less-noteworthy tracks in the Pacific Northwest. He crashed as often as he finished. He finished outside the top ten when he didn't destroy his car. Insurance didn't count for race cars so he was draining the old man's account with vigor.

Now why didn't I think of that? Pops supporting a below-average motorcycle racing career? Because Pops wasn't stupid and I had some pride.

Junior could move up to crashing faster and more expensive cars with a large inheritance. One bigger if Mendez passed away before any of the lawsuits were finalized. Patricide? Pretty strong stuff. I hoped Junior would be present Saturday night and I could evaluate the father-son interaction.

I finished up my notes and wiped my history. I might not get along with computers but I knew enough to leave a minimal trail. Or delude myself I could.

Chapter 14

Friday morning's sky was cloudless and the sun warmed despite the lateness in the year. It was the kind of day visitors checked their wallets to see if they could afford to buy property here. Doing my bit for the Chamber of Commerce, I lowered the Beetle's top and cruised for Pebble Beach sporting sunglasses and a yellow ball cap.

The Moore residence's exterior hadn't improved in a day but there was a man trimming the bushes beside the entrance. I pulled across the road and parked. He was dressed in a sweatshirt with the sleeves cut off, jeans, sneakers and a wide-brimmed straw hat. My shoes crunched the gravel and he glanced.

"Can I help you?"

"I'm looking for Armand Moore. This is his place, right?"

"For now," he said.

"You're him, then?" Two plus two. Doing his own landscaping.

"Yeah. Who wants to know?"

"Clay Farina."

"I don't know you." Armand held the trim shears at chest level. Not a threat, just letting me know it could become one.

"I'll be straight from the start," I said. "I'm a private investigator looking into Oscar Mendez's shooting last February. Checking on as many of his investors as I can."

"Starting with the biggest losers?"

"Something like that." I divided my attention between his expression and the shears. "Do you know anyone who might be angry enough to attack him?"

"I won't incriminate me or anyone else. We'll pursue the bastard legally." He talked using the shears to emphasize.

"Will you and the others get him, legally?"

"Mr. Farina." He pointed toward the house. "Last Christmas Eve, the bank holding my mortgage evicted me and my family. *Christmas Eve.* My daughter was crying as we loaded our presents into the car. She asked me where we were going to have turkey the next day. I couldn't tell her. If I'd wanted to shoot Mendez, that would have been the night to do it."

"Shit. I'm sorry, Mr. Moore. I'm looking for that kind of desperation but not to bring up bad memories for you. How'd you climb back?"

"Friends. Real friends. The kind Mendez will never have. We lease the place, handy for my daughter's school and her friends." He shook his head. "Renting our own house from the bank."

"How old is your girl?"

"Seven."

"Again, shit. Tough time. Glad you know where you'll be celebrating Christmas this year."

"Yeah. Some comfort in the known. Next year, not so certain if we don't settle with Mendez."

"Do you actually meet with any of the other complainants?"

"Not for a few months. Every time we did, the lawyers whacked another percentage point onto their contingency fee. I couldn't pick any out who are likely suspects for you. Neither could the police."

"Did anyone from the Securities Commission ever talk to you?"

"Those assholes? They let Mendez get away with it in the first place. In my opinion, we should be suing them as well."

"Good luck with that."

Moore tipped his hat back. "One thing you should understand, Farina. Most of the anger toward Mendez is really towards ourselves. We made a choice. Driven by greed."

"Driven to help your family, too."

"A rationalization. Greed was the heart. I'll recover, not necessarily my finances, but psychologically. And be more pragmatic in future."

I held out my hand. "I appreciate your candor, Mr. Moore."

He returned the grasp and I handed him my card. "If you hear or remember anything, however minute, especially something or someone out of place, I'd appreciate a call."

He stuffed the card in his rear pocket and returned to the trim task.

I mulled over the things Moore had said on my way further south. I hooked onto the coast highway and headed for Monday's accident scene. Moore had a point, why wait until his life was rebuilding to go after Mendez? Moore seemed like a reasonable guy, emotions directed inward and to his family, not outward to someone beyond his control.

Talking to him, I got a sense of a guy who'd climb back out, remember his friends, move past his enemies and look for an opportunity to pay forward his gratitude. That was today, months after he and his family stood outside their home on Christmas Eve, unable to go back. Today, standing in the sunshine, zenning the shrubbery. A man can mellow out under those conditions. What about after a few ounces of scotch or bourbon? Maybe Mr. Moore and those seemingly resigned think-a-likes became homicidal in their cups. What about his wife? Was she the forgiving, get on with a new life, type? It was cynical, but part of my job.

THE SUN HAD REACHED the treacherous hairpin by the time I arrived. I parked safely off the road and hiked along the ditch to the crash location, camera in hand. I recalled the highway patrol taking pictures of the smashed bike. I assumed they had ones of the tire marks but I couldn't be sure.

A steady stream of cars went past while I stood on the inside of the curve, lowering my position to view the pavement, searching for any remaining tire marks from the crotch rocket. Rain and traffic had weathered the crash marks dim but I could see at least one patch of rubber too narrow for four wheels. When the traffic abated, I clicked a few shots from different angles, using my hat for scale. It was on the right side of the northbound lane. Mine. It had to be the rear; if I'd locked up the front wheel, I wouldn't have remained upright. I replayed Rokon's pass, my slowing and Buddy's ill-fated kick. I'd more than slowed using the BSA's engine to decelerate, I'd pushed the rear brake lever hard. I'd panicked.

A convoy of mega-RV's chased me to the shoulder. What did I have here? Nothing incriminating on either side? I wasn't certain the noise and the buffeting wind as the road barges passed blurred my thoughts. It would still come down to my word or Rokon's. Unless Buddy's conscience weighed in again.

I walked back to my car. San Luis Obispo beckoned but the philandering dentist would have to wait. If he'd sent Steve and Buddy after me in the heat of his guilt revelation, maybe time would cool him off before I paid him a rekindling visit. Thoughts of my own revenge washed through. Key his car? Report him to the dental association? Give him a bad review? My immaturity poured out wish-fulfilling possibilities. Let them emerge, laugh and move on. Leave it in Roger's hands. For now.

I RECOGNIZED THE RED Land Rover in Pops' golf club parking lot. He always parked it in the shade. I had missed the first entrance so I swung in the exit. *Don't arrest me, I plead entitlement.* The Beetle joined his rig in the shade. I trotted up the steps to the bar overlooking the first tee and eighteenth green. No pressure until late in the day when the barflies get vocal. Until some club official in a blazer offers free drinks if they'll shut up.

Pops' back was to me. He, as usual, was toting the final tally. Not the golf scores, per se, but the dollar a shot reward. I grabbed a fifth chair and slipped beside him. I nodded hello to his foursome; Roger Schopff, Milt Canyon and Doc Wills, our retired family physician and all-around good crony.

I watched Pops finish the math. He placed the card on the table between drinks. "You each owe me twenty, Doc gets fifteen each, Roger, the big winner gets forty, and Milt five."

Milt shoved his chair back. As low man, he also had to shout a round. "Same for everyone? Clay, it's on me."

"Lemonade, thanks. I'm driving." I scanned the score card and whispered to Pops. "How come Milt ties for low score but sucks on bingo, bango, bongo?" They get points for longest drive, best approach and longest putt.

Pops whispered back. "He counts well."

Golf-ese for forgetting to add the odd stroke. 'You only cheat yourself', was Pops motto when he tried in vain to foster the passion in me for the game. "I'll be back," I said. "Have to make a phone call."

I used the bar phone to call the hospital and asked for the nurse on Buddy's unit. "Hi, Ms. Figuaredo? It's Clay Farina. I hope this isn't a bad time, I'll only take a minute. Can you tell me who's paying for Buddy Tkachuk's stay? I had no luck with your accounts department."

She said that information was private and normally she wouldn't know but, in this case, she had witnessed a payment when she submitted her overtime ticket. She tagged it because the payment was in cash. Steve Rokon.

"Thanks. How's Buddy doing, by the way?"

No change. Not talking.

I made a second call to Monterey County Sheriff headquarters. "Dennis? It's Clay. Do you have a temporary address for Steve Rokon?"

He gave me the name and location.

"The Can-Am Motel? You rent by the hour or by the month, not many tourists overnight unless they're blind and desperate."

Dennis laughed then hung up.

The Can-Am had seen better days. Not in my lifetime, however. For a guy paying cash for hospital care, it was a budgetary sacrifice. He wasn't paying the bills out of his own pocket.

I listened to the boys kid each other while I washed down an excellent BLT with the lemonade.

Roger said, "You should join us for a round, Clay."

Pops shook his head.

I explained so he didn't have to. "I limit my father's embarrassment to one round a year. Where no one knows us. We had our game in August."

"Castroville," said Pops. "We can't go back."

"It wasn't that bad, Pops." Then I thought more. Yeah, it had been. I tallied. One broken window, that's what you get for living on a course. Multiple divots, they don't mind the fairway ones or even the tee box but the ones on the green are strictly verboten. Plowing the cart into a sand trap; I swear I had the brake set.

Roger cornered me after lunch in the parking lot. "I spoke with Elizabeth's doctor. We can meet with her Monday at her office."

I wrote the address down. "Thanks, Roger. Here's an interesting tidbit. Steve Rokon is paying Buddy's hospital bills in cash."

"Unusual, it must drive the hospital controller nuts in the age of electronic transfers. It creates an advantage for whoever is really footing the bill."

"Untraceable, that's my thought."

I left the quartet to replay their game in the parking lot and headed for the Can-Am.

I PARKED ACROSS THE street, in a strip mall facing the Can-Am Motel. Free WIFI and Cable TV were big selling points, though it actually read Fr_e WIFI and Cabl_; someone had stolen the 'e's. The mall had everything Rokon would need, given his wheels were in traction. Laundromat, convenience/liquor store and a nail and hair salon. Free wine with each manicure and beer with a hair cut. Classy.

Watching my step, the deck shoes were relatively new, I jaywalked into the motel's lot. I guessed two of the four cars hadn't run or moved in months, judging by the guano and salt buildup.

The bell spring over the office door announced my entry. A red-eyed clerk in a neatly pressed apron skirt and white blouse appeared from a nook behind the counter. The name tag read Frecia. No one had stolen the 'e'.

"Yes sir? You wish the room?"

Her Latino accent was charming. I hoped she didn't have to pull the night shift and deal with inebriated customers who thought it was inviting rather than charming.

"I'm actually looking for a friend. From San Luis Obispo. Rokon?"

"Oh, yes. Mister Rokon, he is in room 12. I don't think he here right now. You leave a message?" She pushed a motel pad and logo'd pen to me.

"How does he get around? After the crash?"

"Mister Rokon sometime take the taxi. Today he walks." She pushed the pad a bit closer.

"I'll catch him another time." I passed her twenty bucks. "You don't need to tell Mister Rokon I was here."

The twenty disappeared in a blur. "Room 12," she said.

I checked the sight lines for room 12 and recrossed the road. The convenience store provided a newspaper and parking for the afternoon.

Colin Marsh's third installment on the Rudge affair delved into the societal cost stemming from domestic abuse. Acceptance from the lack of will to denounce the behavior. The police didn't escape Colin's blame either. Too often, though not in this case because Elizabeth had never contacted authorities, repeated warnings from police did little to change the behavior of the abuser. Colin finished with the admonition 'Silence is the enemy. Remain so and your guilt is assured.' Monday's column would feature the other half of the Rudge accusation. Oscar Mendez and his rise to fame and infamy.

Dusk descended and I moved the Beetle to a corner in the motel's lot. I didn't want to spook my quarry enough to move. I liked knowing where he was settled for the moment but I wanted to know where he spent his time outside the motel.

At half-past six, a Peninsula Taxi cab showed up and dropped Steve off in the strip mall. I almost missed him. He paid the driver and went into the convenience store. I noted the taxi's details and then watched my target emerge with a grocery sack. I snapped two pictures in the inadequate lighting. He was unsteady, drunk or high, but made it to the motel without being run over.

I was hungry, stiff and disappointed. I couldn't think of any reason to engage Steve and come out a winner. Not tonight, not in private.

The cab company's office wasn't far from my route home and I dropped in. Forty bucks and ten minutes later, I had Steve's pickup point. The Silver Sardine. Rowdy, decent food, not a great pickup bar, patrons trended in groups, but if frottage was your thing, on Friday and Saturday nights it was usually packed tighter than a tin of fish. It would have to wait until Monday for a visit from me. The pictures might help i.d. Steve to the staff, if they'd talk.

I also gleaned his bank's location. NorCal Savings & Loan. I wasn't sure how I'd get any details there; bank employees are committed to privacy. But if the dentist's bank in San Luis Obispo was the same, I'd have one more tenuous link. Put enough such links together and I'd have a tenuous chain.

My balcony helped to put a period on day's end. Morning would entail reshuffling my suspect card deck with today's input. Grilled bass and chilled chardonnay while listening to the waves peeled the stress layers away.

Chapter 15

I re-organized my cards and pinned them to my corkboard in five pyramids. Mendez family. A three-card effort. Him atop and wife and Oscar Jr. below. Beside it, Mendez business. Oscar atop and unknown partners and associates below. Public record scrutiny of his various companies and Pops input required there, if Mendez trusted anyone to be partners.

Next came Elizabeth Rudge and family. Jolene, her brother and Gordon on the second line, Tiffany underneath. The next class was the largest. Investors. Not a pyramid but columns. I had one for individuals and one for institutions, the latter blank cards for now until Farina-Black provided some wealth manager names.

The fifth and final area had one card. Percy Oaks from the Securities Commission.

I stepped back to survey the names and begin sketching connections. If I didn't see them immediately, having the wall in my peripheral vision every time I walked past could jar an unseen link into focus.

I pink-stickered those who had reason to shoot Mendez and yellowed those with a possible motive to frame Elizabeth for the deed. The list of overlap would keep me busy a few days observing and researching in depth.

A call to the marina provided a close-enough-for-jazz estimate of Gordon Rudge's slip and moorage fees. Add running expense for one or two outings a week, fixed costs for food, drink and Tiffany. The total was significant. The man was either still generating income or his burn rate was covered by substantial principal. He'd been hiding funds from

Elizabeth while they were still married, I guessed, anticipating a costly divorce settlement or avoiding taxes by washing funds offshore or a myriad of less obvious reasons. In any case, his losses to Mendez hurt Elizabeth more than him. Though he cried a different story.

I checked some power yacht prices. He couldn't buy more than a studio apartment for what his was worth, and there was always a greater surplus of boats than real estate for sale. His monthly fees could cover a substantial apartment rent, with an ocean view. Maybe. The man's vocal displeasure at living on a boat wasn't justified, in my opinion. I didn't think he had motive for either attacking Mendez or fingering his ex-wife so I folded both his stickers for now. Tiffany's yellow I left. The anger toward Gordon's ex might not be financial in her case; emotion could be stronger.

Jolene Rudge's pink sticker needed more research too. A visit to her facility to get a sense of prosperity could be tomorrow's outing. If things went well tonight with Ynez, a drive over the hills into Salinas Valley could be the perfect excuse.

Elizabeth's pink sticker matched her daughter's, with more motive. She had lost a decent chunk of her settlement to the scammer. Monday's interview with her psychiatrist might give me stronger evidence one way or the other. The one thing against her was the decline in her aim. She'd hit a running husband with every shot. Mendez's attacker was only two for five.

Mendez Sr. had no stickers. His son and wife had pink but they were provisional since I didn't know enough about either. The son spent in high volume but relied on his father's steady income stream. Stopping it with a bullet or five wouldn't be a long-term solution. If he was smart enough to understand.

That left me with Armand Moore and his fellow investors. A big swath. And the unknown institutional managers keeping heads down. The list from Pops would add names and complicate my future.

My speculations had taken me past noon. Tonight's dinner would be late, for me. I would sample the fare at The Silver Sardine and pray I didn't get food poisoning. I wanted to see how much of a splash Steve Rokon, small spender, was making.

THE SARDINE'S ONE O'CLOCK crowd wasn't worthy of the term. Was the bar half empty or half full? I opted for half full and took a table beside four well-geared motorcyclists. I nodded and said, "Those your Beemers outside?" The bikes had road dirt in abundance.

"Yeah. Don't take a picture until we clean them." A guy with full beard and raccoon eyes.

"Don't worry. One of the reasons I try not to ride in the rain is the time it takes to clean every inch. Especially the spokes. One at a time." My beer arrived and I toasted. "Keeping the rubber side down. Where you coming from and where you headed?"

"Alaska," said one of the women. "Heading home to Redondo Beach. We'll take a few more days. This is as far as we come today. Work can always wait, right?"

Her helmet sported an insect graveyard. She drove one of them.

"Do you switch up?" I pointed at her helmet.

The other woman nodded. "Passenger life can get boring after the first two thousand miles."

"Driving's thirstier," I said. "Changing up lets somebody enjoy a beer or two on the road. Be careful in the morning on the coast road. It's the time of year for icy spots first thing."

"The waitress was just telling me about an accident earlier in the week. One guy went down hard." Their meals arrived and the talk ran down.

The waitress turned to me, pencil ready. I asked, "If you were me, what would you order?"

"I recommend the clubhouse."

"Thank you. I will have the clubhouse sandwich. What were they saying about a bike accident?"

"There's a guy comes in the last three or four nights. Willing to show anyone his leg burn for a free beer. It's disgusting."

"Is he a tall guy, blond hair, goes by Steve?"

"That'd be him."

"What's he say about the accident? And his passenger."

"He says they were racing another bike. Hot shoe rider. Tried to take him on a curve and leaned over too much. Scraped pegs and flipped."

I didn't want to put words in her mouth but I had to know. "Did he say anything else about the second bike?"

"Nope. Just bragging he kept up with the guy who knew the road."

"You gotta be careful. There's always someone better than you."

"Or worse," she said.

"Since we have this business arrangement for the next hour or two, what do I call you besides, 'hey you'?"

"Chevonne."

"I'm Clay. And I'll have a salad with my sandwich instead of fries."

"I'd recommend the fries," she said. "The lettuce is a shade wilted."

"Agreed. And a round for my well-traveled friends."

The four quickly drained their beers.

Dennis would need to speak with Chevonne if Steve's charges held up.

The clubhouse wasn't bad. I gave it 6 out of 10 but the information got a 9.

Chapter 16

Ynez looked stunning with her hair twisted high and dressed in a colorful wrap which hung below her knees. I was glad I chose a tux, at least my outfit kept pace. We drove through the country club gates and a valet took charge of the Beetle. "No racing," I told him with a smile.

"No, sir. Not our m.o."

"I'm kidding. Henson's long gone, isn't he."

"A blight on the trade, sir."

I reached for my pocket but he stopped me. "No tipping allowed, sir. Another policy we follow."

I cleared my throat and offered Ynez my arm. "That could've been awkward," I said.

"What was the reference to Henson? I assume not the same guy that created the Muppets."

"No. This Henson was a valet service used by many of the clubs and upscale wharf restaurants. A few customers got suspicious when their GPS trackers showed their cars were driven to the lot the long way. Joy-ridden. The popularity of dashcams revealed more visual proof."

She stopped. "That's just stupid."

"Agreed. You can't always trust the people working for you have the same long-term vision of building a solid reputation. Henson found out the hard way."

We resumed walking and passed a cluster of propane heaters warming outside tables. The main lobby was decorated with large picture posters featuring immigrant families' testimonials. I scanned for Pops and mom, then for Mendez. He was on an elevated platform, chatting enthusiastically with other guests.

Oscar Mendez Sr. was shorter and chunkier than I'd imagined. I recognized his wife. She was tall and lithe and prettier than her photos.

Before I could search for the son, I heard our names called.

"Ynez, Clay."

"Mother." I greeted her with a cheek kiss and Ynez did the same.

"Wendy," said Ynez. "This is quite the gala. Anyone else we both know present?"

"Thankfully not," mom replied. "No faculty gossip tonight. You must get a drink." Mom pointed her to the traveling servers long enough to whisper, "Does Ynez know you're working tonight? You've seen Mr. Mendez."

"No, she does not. I'm not working, I'm merely observing. Though I'd like to meet him."

"I know Cecile. Mrs. Mendez. Come on." Mom grabbed my arm and pulled me toward the Mendez receiving line. I nodded to Felicia Diaz as we passed the Herald's editor.

We mounted the stage and mom released my arm. I continued, drawn in her wake.

"Cecile, how nice to see you. I don't think you've met my son, Clay."

"Wendy, hello. Mr. Farina. A pleasure."

The smile and voice were as smooth as her looks. Cecile Mendez didn't try to be elegant; she just was.

"My husband, Oscar." She transferred my hand from her delicate but firm clasp to her husband's. Indelicate and strong.

"Clay Farina," I said. "This is an impressive undertaking on your part."

"Thank you. Are you in business with your father? He is a well-respected man and a great supporter of our work with recent immigrants."

He finally released my hand, worse for the experience. I winced inside but resisted the urge to stick it in a cold drink. "I work with Pops but not in a wealth management role."

"Isn't it the way with offspring, Wendy?" he said. "They enjoy the fruits of our labors but often follow a different passion. My namesake, he has no passion for serving the people, only racing them. And at that, he fails too often." Mendez shrugged as if Junior's disappointing lack of self-supporting career was inevitable.

"I wish I could have lived up to Pops' hopes of a dynasty. Turns out I didn't have the aptitude. Better to serve him in a different capacity which I'm good at and enjoy."

"That is?" His eyes focused on mine. Mendez probably knew when people were telling him the truth by watching their eyes.

"I pursue information. Protect his clients if needed. Discourage those who would harm the firm or its patrons."

"You are security."

"In a word, yes."

"That is good. A man needs to feel secure. For himself and his family. It was nice meeting you."

I had met, disgorged the fact that I was of no further use, therefore interest, to him.

"Thanks, mom." We made our way back to the main floor.

"Now you can concentrate on Ynez."

I laughed. "Well done. I'd still like to get a look at Oscar Jr.."

"I haven't seen him yet. There's Glen and Ynez. Let's see if she needs rescuing."

YNEZ AND I DID OUR mock evaluations of the silent auction items. Trips, lessons, antiques, art, high-end fashions. They were impressive, the donors getting reasonable publicity, the buyers the same plus something they might otherwise have ignored. And a tax break.

"What do you think of this?" Ynez held up a sheer piece of lingerie.

"Slow down, tiger," I said. "I'm not wearing that on the first or second date." I moved on before I had a heart attack. She was still laughing.

The next travel item caught my eye. Desert and dirt bikes.

Ynez read the description aloud. "Baja Experience of a Lifetime. Five days guided riding through Mexico."

I wrote my name and a stupid bid before she'd finished. Stupid low. "You'd like this?"

It wasn't disbelief in her voice. It was surprise, not at the trip but I sensed more at me.

"Absolutely, even if I only made it to sundown on the first day. I mean, I haven't thrown my leg over a dirt bike in ten years but I ride on the street nearly every day."

"Tell me, one of those noise and chrome jobs with an engine twice the size of my van's?"

"No. Something even older than your van." I tried to keep the jargon to a minimum as I explained the rise, fall and resurrection of the British motorcycle industry and my part in renewing the second-generation cottage trade around remanufactured vintage items.

"I get it, you're not one of the doo-rag set."

"Hey, there's room on the road for all enthusiasts." Except when two bikes try to occupy the same point in space. A hairpin on the Pacific Coast Highway.

"Mr. Farina, nice to see you again."

I turned and greeted Felicia Diaz. "Ms. Diaz, good evening. This is Ynez Jones, Environmental Studies, Cal Sate Monterey, in case you need it for the caption."

"What's he talking about?" Ynez asked her.

Felicia explained. "I edit the County Herald. I'm not here reporting. I'm here supporting. Among other ties, my paper's distributor is a Vietnamese family business who got their start due to Mr. Mendez's efforts to convince me to hire them when my previous provider retired."

"No pictures tonight?" I asked. "I wore my tux for nothing?"

"Colin is around somewhere, I'll put in a word for you when I see him." She drifted away.

"I now know your passion for two wheels, tell me how you tie in to your father's business."

"Only after you tell me about the environment and where it ends."

We drifted past more auction items and descriptions. The bid sheets were filling up. By the time we'd circled back to Baja Adventure, Ynez had filled my head with environmental emergencies, solutions and ongoing efforts. "Education is the only real long-term solution."

"I'll concede that," I said. "Education, but not continual wolf cries. The people you need to educate quit listening when they're overwhelmed by fanatics preaching the world will end tomorrow. Then it doesn't."

"I know. Climate psychologists are trying to change the way the information is presented to get around our brains' protective shields. Bring it closer, make change simple and convenient. Alter the easy behaviors. But I should get down from my soapbox."

"Don't worry. I don't envy your task but I admire it."

I saw Oscar Mendez Jr. for the first time. He hovered over the Baja bid sheet. He looked around and I ensured I wasn't staring. When I swept my gaze past him, I saw the top bid sheet disappear into his pocket. He wrote on the next paper. He left and I waited until he was out of sight before guiding Ynez past it.

His was the only bid on the sheet. Mine had vanished. What surprised me was his bid was lower than mine had been. I'd wait until the final ring before checking it again.

Ynez said, "What happened to your bid?"

"Not everyone here is an altruist."

"You mean shithead."

"Yeah." I laughed. "That would be the scientific term."

"Now it's your turn to tell me the tale of Clay Farina and his chosen career."

"When I realized higher finance wasn't my thing, I was in my final year at university. I'd minored in justice studies and considered using my undergrad degree to enter law school but three more years of academia was too much. Lawyers work too hard and police suffer more challenges than my temperament allows. Private security offered the flexibility that suited me best. I happened to have a couple of early successes working for Pops and Farina-Black retains me because of my track record and not my father's influence."

The dinner gong sounded and I escorted Ynez to the main dining hall. Pops' table had filled up except for our two seats. I saw the Mendez clan at the very front.

My knees buckled. I lost footing and heard a 'crack'. Not a bone. The ground. Ynez stumbled into me. "Jonas was right," I said. "We're sliding into the ocean." I yelled to Pops. "Outside."

I grabbed Ynez around the waist and pulled mom to her feet. Pops had mom's other arm and the four of us moved toward the exit. When the three of them were on the turf, I returned to the doors. "Move as quickly as you can," I shouted. "Leave your stuff behind. Get out of the building."

The swaying had stopped but after-tremors were likely on their way. "Don't go back inside. There may be more 'quakes to come." Oscar Jr. and his wife bolted past me, followed by Mendez the elder, unencumbered by Cecile. A handful of men and women wandered solo across the grass, calling names. Milt Canyon was going the wrong way. "Milt, stay out here."

"Sharon was in the washroom, I've got to find her."

"Here she comes," I said.

I saw them re-unite though her look wasn't entirely grateful. Pops' table had eight people seated before the earthquake hit. Sharon Canyon had been among them. Milt had panicked. Like Mendez Sr. and half a dozen other spouses.

Club security had taken charge now and manned the entrances. I rejoined the Farina family.

"Everyone at our table accounted for?"

Pops nodded.

"That brought some excitement to an otherwise rather dull soiree," my mother said.

"Do we get a rain check?" I asked.

"Don't be glib, Clay."

"Following your lead, mother."

"Hush, you two," said Pops. "The club chairman is trying to get everyone's attention."

We quieted. Without the benefit of a PA system, the spokesman had to yell. "I've been assured by staff that everyone is accounted for. After-shocks may continue for some time so any valuables abandoned inside will be secured by staff once they get the all-clear from emergency services. Obviously, the auction will be delayed. We'll arrange alternate bid closure this week when normalcy returns. Please leave your contact information with my secretary who is setting up as I speak." He pointed to a man seated at a patio table beside him. "Phone service appears to be unaffected so if you have family to call and haven't, please go ahead. I thank you all for coming out tonight and we will meet again all in person next year. Mr. Mendez, would you care to add anything?"

Oscar Sr. took the limelight. He looked as shaken as the earth. I wondered if the sound wave had reminded him too much of the gunshots he'd heard when attacked. Didn't excuse the son from foregoing the 'women and children first' credo.

"I too wish to add my thanks for you coming out tonight. I'm sorry we will not be able to enjoy the fabulous meal. I urge you all to partake in the auction once we are able to resume the process, most likely online?" He looked to the chairman for confirmation. A nod. "Yes. Keep watching the Foundation's website."

Servers were emerging from the fairway bar with beer and wine.

"Well," I said. "We may go hungry but we won't go thirsty."

Ynez squeezed my arm. "Thanks for taking charge in there. I was lost for a moment. Confused."

"Remember what we said about the world not ending tomorrow?"

"This wasn't pollution, this was an act of nature," she said.

"It points to the root cause of both eventual outcomes, though."

"What do you mean?"

"People living in or creating harm's way because there's too many of us to be able to choose only the safe places to live and the safe ways to live. I'll step down from my soapbox now. Let's enjoy what we can from the company we keep."

She grabbed two beer while mom accepted glasses and a bottle of grunt. "Let's find a table," said Pops.

There was one minor after-shock an hour later. By then, cabs were rolling up to ferry us home. The four of us crammed in one. Unluckily, for me, Ynez's digs were the closest. I bade her a warm and chaste good night.

"I'll pick you up tomorrow and we'll retrieve your car?" she asked.

"Deal, thank you. How'd you like to take a cruise up Carmel Valley and over the mountains into Salinas?" Another reason for the excursion popped into my head. I wouldn't exploit Ynez's presence but she might make my subsidiary task go smoother.

"I'd like that. What time should I come to your place?"

"Ten?"

"See you then, Clay. And thanks again for an adrenaline-fuelled evening."

"I try to be memorable."

We dropped the folks off and I got stuck with the fare. I counted the drinks at the club and guessed it was a wash.

My building looked sound. Another minor seismic event. The minor ones were good, they said, kept the continental plates moving past each other without getting stuck prior to the big one. I had one message.

"Clay, it's Jonas. Told you so."

"In harm's way," I said aloud.

Chapter 17

Pops had me out of bed and on the road at six on Sunday morning. We celebrated the early Sabbath by ferrying vehicles from the previous night's bash to their owners, courtesy of Farina-Black and the valet service. Pops didn't view it as self-promotion, but as his good deed for the day. We didn't wake anyone who wasn't up. Keys were left securely inside locked cars, pushed through the mail slot or delivered in person if someone stirred. My Beetle was the last rescued. I lowered the top, hopped in and bid Pops a good morning.

I showered and fed in the nick of time for Ynez's pickup.

We met on the street. "'Morning," I greeted. "I'm not trying to be gallant, but it's looks like a convertible day." I explained the Farina valet service while I opened the garage door. "Why don't you park inside and we'll take the Beetle. I can be your tour guide for places you haven't explored yet."

"Deal." She fished a ball cap from the rear of her van. I did the parking dance, 'watch out for the bike' was easier to say if you didn't have to say it at all.

Headgear affixed, we drove through Monterey. "Did you have any trouble on the roads?" I asked.

"A couple of fallen trees and one retaining wall by my place which crumbled over the sidewalk into the curb lane. I didn't see a single emergency vehicle."

"It was minor, even for this area. Were other parts of the state hit? I haven't heard news since Pops dragged me forth into the day."

"No, we were it. We'll be on the national news every hour on the hour, until a better story comes along."

I short-cutted in Del Monte onto the feeder road to the valley highway. Some traffic signals were on four-way flash but traffic was light and we got cruising comfortably in no time. I pointed out various landmarks and then turned off the main road to go over the hills and down into Salinas Valley. When we reached the summit, I could hear the far away buzz of high-revving engines.

The buzz waxed and waned like a band of hornets as we drove closer to Laguna Seca's main gates. "Church service for petrolheads," I explained.

"Have you ever tried the circuit?"

"Did a track day on my BSA the first year after its restoration."

"And no more?"

"Every Spring I take a road-skills tune up course for a day. I don't race; I'd rather spend my days riding and not repairing the previous weekend's learning curve." I pulled into the guest lot, stopped and dug into my wallet. "I get a pass for non-sanctioned events. Come on, let's have a bite of lunch and watch the action." I thought of another information bird I could kill as well.

I parked in the paddock and we grabbed hot dogs and lemonade and found a spot to watch the cars prep for the next race.

"How do you not go deaf?" Ynez asked when two high-strung Austin-Healey Sprites tore past at half the speed they sounded.

"Earplugs. I can run back to the pit and get a pair."

"It's not bad here but if we spend any time closer to the action, I will demand protection."

I dug for a clean tissue. "Here, roll up enough to wad in and learn to read lips."

We both did and then finished our missiles of death. "On to Salinas," I shouted.

On our way to the car, I spotted a track marshal I knew from my times at the course. "Ed, you're working the small timers today."

"Hi, Clay. There are no small-timers, only small engines." He spoke to me but his eyes were on Ynez.

"This is my friend, Ynez. Ynez, this be Ed."

"He's not trying to convince you to be his pit crew, is he?" Ed asked.

She held up the make-do earplugs in her palm. "Too noisy, give me an afternoon on the ocean, listening to birds and waves."

Ed looked at her in disbelief but kept his thoughts non-verbal.

"Ed," I asked, "do you know Oscar Mendez Jr.?"

"I have watched Junior cause his share of wrecks. I have berated him, disqualified him and observed him in disbelief. But I do not know him. Why?"

"I think you just answered my next question about his character. Third question, despite his on-track behavior, is he any good? Or would he be if he wasn't an ass?"

"No, he isn't. Doesn't know machinery, other than in one of two states, working under the lash of his foot or broken. He doesn't take the time to adapt to track conditions or competition level. There should be a special class for dilettantes with more money than skill."

"Tell me how you really feel?" I squeezed Ed's shoulder.

"You should come out for the vintage fun-runs. Your Goldstar is a thoroughbred and needs to be let out of the barn on occasion."

"I'm flattered. Can I call on you as an expert witness for a possible case?"

"Yes." Ed's attention went to the track and he ran off.

He grabbed a yellow flag and jumped a fence to wave down two approaching cars.

"What happened?" Ynez asked.

"He heard the crash." I pointed in a ninety-degree angle from where he stood, frantically slowing cars down. "He reacted while I was still processing the information. Come on, let's go find a different kind of thoroughbred."

"What do you mean? More race jargon I don't understand?"

"No. The four-legged kind. A recent acquaintance runs a stable in the Salinas Valley. I'd like to take a look. Are you game?"

"If I don't have to climb up on a horse, yes."

I CHECKED MY MAP BEFORE we headed down from the hills. Jolene's operation would be six miles further inland from a landmark I knew.

An iron arch over the driveway read J & L Stables. A second sign, just inside the gateway, advertised Riding Academy and Boarding.

"Who or what are J & L?" Ynez asked.

"I'm pretty sure the 'J' is for Jolene Rudge. The 'L' is a partner?" Business, personal or both? Jolene hadn't mentioned a partner and I got the impression she was working seven days a week with little time off for good behavior. Her brother Lawrence was an 'L'. Simple was usually right but nothing in this case so far had appeared simple.

There were two horse trailers in the parking lot, one hitched to a high-end Land Rover, the other to a Lamborghini SUV. I had to check the hood badge for its identity. I'd never seen one, let alone held a mortgage for one. The odds were good Jolene did work her saddle cushion off but she could charge gold for it.

Six other vehicles half-filled the lot. I could see mounted riders circling in two corrals to our left. We walked up s flight of steps set into turf. There stood a larger arena set up with jumps. It was empty so we made for the barn.

Young girls groomed mounts outside the stable row. A cheerful geezer in a red blazer and well-worn jeans passed along the enthusiasts carrying two buckets in each hand.

"Maybe this is 'L'," I said.

We waited for him to distribute his loads then I waved to him.

He trotted over. Around his neck hung a garish scrap of frayed cloth.

"Sunday tie?" I asked.

"I wear ties every day," he said. "Make 'em myself. Ties by Samuel. That's me, Samuel T. Washburn. Might get one of them websites and sell 'em." He fingered it tenderly. "But you're right, this is my Sunday tie. There was a young lady in church this morning couldn't take her eyes off me." He winked at Ynez.

"Who wouldn't," she said. "I think it's lovely and I like a man who dresses up."

"You're awfully kind, miss."

A shout from the ring drew his attention. "They need me."

"Where can we find Jolene?"

Samuel pointed to a steel building behind the two corrals. "Indoor arena," he said. He trotted off with a limp.

My estimation of Jolene's character went up a notch. Samuel was no geezer; he was a forty-something body whose mind hadn't caught up in age. One of those people you couldn't help but like. Neither was he the 'L.'

It took a minute for my eyes to adjust to the dim interior but there was no mistaking the smell. Horse crap and money. Horse upkeep was their weight in dollars every month. At least, that was how I reckoned the boarding, lessons and incidentals. Two riders circled inside. The lead was Jolene. A smaller version of her in black helmet, top, boots and white breeches followed in her wake.

Jolene's commands were sharp and brooked no nonsense. She pulled her mount to the inside. "You lead," she instructed. She didn't give us a second glance as she rode past our viewpoint. The commands kept coming, corrections interspersed with praise and encouragement. A distant klaxon chimed. I checked my watch. Two o'clock.

"Okay, Miranda. We're done. Cool off on the outer path and make sure she's groomed and settled for the night. I've got you down for Tuesday after school. We still good?"

"Yes, Ms. Rudge."

Jolene approached us. "What brings you here?"

"We were in the neighborhood?"

She didn't appreciate my humor.

"Ynez is a recent addition to the area and hadn't seen the wonders of the Salinas Valley. I offered to be her guide. Ynez Jones, this is Jolene Rudge."

The two exchanged pleasantries but Jolene was still hunting for an explanation.

I said, "I wanted to see your ranch. I, we, are very impressed."

"It must be a lot of work," said Ynez. "You have to manage people, horses and the facility. Does 'L' help?"

Words stolen from my mouth. Good job, Ynez.

"'L' is my brother Lawrence, most times. He is a silent partner."

"Other times?"

"The 'L' stands for luck, of which you need plenty; and love, you have to have passion for what you do. I know it looks impressive and I work very hard to keep ahead or abreast of my competition. If I'm not improving, I'm falling behind. I employ the best instructors I can and charge enough to make a reasonable profit at the end of each month. I don't have time for idle chit-chat." She rode past us. "Look around all you want, just don't get in the way."

"Who's Samuel?" I asked.

She stopped and turned in the saddle. "My right hand. He keeps the facility in top shape, helps with the boarding and reminds me we're not all given the same chance starting out in life." Jolene resumed her retreat from us.

Amen. "Seen enough?" I asked my date.

Ynez nodded. "This isn't my wheelhouse. I have a request."

"Ask away."

"We passed a Farmer's Market sign up the highway. I shall purchase the ingredients for a tasty Jones and Company supper."

"I'm in. I think all they sell are vegetables."

"No problem. You will be amazed at what I can do with vegetables, mushrooms, spices and wine."

"I'm all in."

"THAT WAS SPECTACULAR," I said. "I may give up meat." Never fish, though, my body demanded seafood.

"Thank you. Your wine choice was excellent."

"We are privileged to be on the doorstep of many great regions for the fermented grape. I'm going to stop at two glasses but I will open a second bottle for you and not begrudge." I didn't want to drive on any more and it was not the night to escalate our relationship, if we had one.

Her reaction was a smile and a chuckle. "I understand and I agree. Too soon."

Agreement it may be, it was still awkward. "I hope you didn't mind my combining business with our pleasure tour today. It happened to be convenient to visit the track and the equestrian center. I'm working for Jolene's mother and wished to know more about the daughter."

Ynez tucked in her long legs and held out her glass. "Did you learn anything? Unveil an important clue?"

I poured and resisted the temptation to say the hell with taking things slow and driving myself home. "I don't know. My process is to process. I'm usually right on first impressions of people but not always of data. It takes retrospection to fit the pieces together."

"What was your impression of Jolene Rudge?"

"It's the third time I've met her. The first was a confrontation in my office after the article came out on her mother. The second was in the company of her father, divorced from the mother and lastly, today. In her most normal environment. Some traits are consistent. She's focused, whether it be to protect family or to tutor her riding students. What do you think, having met only once?"

"I'd say she's honest and doesn't hide her emotions."

"Her dislike toward me isn't disguised."

"I don't know if I'd call it dislike. Mistrust?"

"Either way, I'm not on her most welcome list. Let's backtrack. You observed Oscar Jr. last night and heard Ed's evaluation today. Consistent?"

"Too easy, if you ask me. The prodigal son anything but. Not a surprise, but can you blame him?"

"You're right, the oak and the acorn."

"Or he's been indulged all his life. Told he was the best at this and that, even though he was far from it. Hear it early, and enough, and you believe it."

"Poor guy. Born into wealth and privilege and turns out to be a prick. At some point, one becomes an adult and makes appropriate choices."

"Was your father always...prosperous?"

"No, not when I was little. We gained wealth gradually, it was never a leap from one plateau to the next. I never thought much about it until he made me pay my own way through college."

"But he did facilitate your career."

"Yeah, he did. I tell myself and those who'll listen that I earned that career but it's hard not to get out from Farina-Black's umbrella. Though I have done occasional work outside the firm. And been successful."

Ynez set her empty glass down. She waved off my offer to refill. "No, thanks. I have to be on stage tomorrow."

"How modest was your upbringing?"

Ynez sank into the cushions. "We kind of went the other way. I remember luxury as a child. A huge house until I was four, then we downsized more than once. By the time I reached high school, we rented a carriage house from my aunt and uncle in Oxnard. I was fortunate to get scholarships to supplement university costs. I'm still paying off student loans but I can see daylight, if I'm able to stick with Cal State."

"What caused the decline, if you don't mind telling me?"

"Bad luck and misjudgment. My dad had a paving company with solid contracts in a few counties. His partner embezzled the firm and ran off with the company's bookkeeper. Dad refused to seek bankruptcy and spent ten years paying back every sub-contractor who got stuck. We had champagne when the last one was zeroed. I was fifteen and sick for three days."

"I am impressed beyond words," I said.

There was silence for a good five minutes while Ynez stared, unfocused past me and out her window. When she came back to the present, I took it as my cue.

"I will call you this week. I may have to clean up some unfinished business in San Luis Obispo."

"I'll let you do that road trip on your own."

"Are your folks still in Oxnard?"

"No. Dad took a position with Pismo Beach road maintenance five years ago and they live modestly but in their own home again."

We kissed at her van and exchanged 'good nights' and 'thank you's'.

I began to plan my week on the way home. Monday loomed with meeting Elizabeth's psychiatrist. I hoped Roger had unearthed some useful information on Buddy and Steve as well.

I had my third glass of wine sitting on my balcony watching the stars and sea.

Chapter 18

I read Monday's paper while I waited for Roger to show up at Dr. Tam's office. The Oscar Mendez story ran immediately below the earth tremor coverage on the Herald's front page. A photo taken at the fundraiser of Mendez tied the two together. Editor Felicia Diaz penned the lead article, relating her first-hand experience at the auction. Colin Marsh's byline was on the latter.

Colin's profile on the developer/promoter/speculator began with Mendez's early successes. He'd used his father's real estate holdings as collateral. Mendez started buying discounted commercial property and turning a profit within a few years. His model was to lease back-end-loaded space. Cheap up front but it turned half-empty strip malls into fully-occupied ones. Prosperous appearance became reality. As the trade increased, so did their rents. He'd flip the properties when he reached a target threshold, usually ten percent per year, so in five years he'd realize a sixty percent minimum gain. His investors saw half of it. The money he'd pledge for the next round wouldn't be his but other investors wanting to cash in on the potential return.

Housing developments and office complexes were the next logical step and their details followed the same pattern. Government oversight would be the focus of Wednesday's column. I looked forward to it. So far, Mendez had been portrayed as an opportunist with impeccable timing, building a track record and making himself rich. Was there collusion or were regulatory grey areas and inaction enough?

"I'm glad Elizabeth is out of their crosshairs." Roger sat down with his own paper.

"I wonder if they're finished with her. Her last week, Mendez this week, perhaps the joint connections next week."

"All the more reason for us to push on quickly. By the way, Mendez pays his contractors on time and in full."

"He's smart enough to know how to treat those guys. Nothing like a bulldozer coming through your front gate at midnight to speed up a 'check lost in the mail.'" One category eliminated from the suspect wall.

I changed gears. "Did you find anything on my bikers?"

"Yes. I'll brief you after we talk with Dr. Tam."

On cue, a petite woman in a business suit opened the door to her office. "Mr. Schopff and Mr. Farina. I'm Wendy Tam. Sorry to keep you waiting. Please come in."

I estimated her age to be fifty but it was hard to tell. She had the ageless, smooth skin of a Vietnamese but her eyelids wrinkled the makeup when she blinked.

"You told my receptionist you wished to speak in general terms about Elizabeth Rudge. Correct?"

Roger nodded. "For the moment, general is all I can ask, given your confidentiality bonds."

"Most of my evaluation is in the public record for her parole."

I nodded. "We've both reviewed the official files but words don't always convey tone, if you know what I mean."

Tam looked at me. "I know Mr. Schopff by reputation but what is your involvement, Mr. Farina?"

"Last week's Herald published an anonymous accusation connecting Elizabeth to the attack on Oscar Mendez last February. Specifically linking a similar pistol to the one she used on her husband five years ago. I'm investigating other possibilities Mr. Schopff can use in defense if the charges are pursued by the police and D.A.."

Roger took up the narrative. "You could be called as a witness to state of mind by me or the prosecution. I'd like to know if you're more valuable to my case as a friend or as a hostile for the opposition."

Dr. Tam frowned. "I appreciate your candor, Mr. Schopff. Should I have my own attorney present?"

"You may at the point when things get serious. At the moment, Clay and I are more interested in your assessment of Elizabeth's state of mind when you completed your evaluation. Was she bitter, contrite, unlikely to ever re-offend?"

"We know you gave her a healthy report," I said. "The public record, as you mentioned. More jailtime wasn't going to make a difference. But did you have any misgivings at all about the risk of publicity or running into her ex-husband or his allies in the divorce?"

"I did not. She was the victim in the marriage and the shooting, in my opinion. Once she accepted that her self-guilt wasn't justified, she adopted a calmer outlook. With each passing month after her release, I watched her gain confidence in building a new life for herself."

"No hidden resentment around the loss of status and wealth?" I asked.

"If there was, it was well hidden. I mean, she would occasionally express a wish to travel more but the lack of a companion seemed to hold her back rather than finances."

Roger opened the paper on Tam's desk. "Did she ever mention Oscar Mendez? By name or profession?"

Tam scanned the article. "Mr. Mendez. His foundation helped friends of mine. When they returned the favor, by investing in his schemes, they lost money. Not everything, but enough to induce them to work even harder."

"Did you invest?" I asked.

"I thought I was helping his cause. His efforts weren't yet established in my time. When I immigrated from Vietnam, it took three years for my credentials to be recognized to the point of writing examinations. I worked as a cleaner in a car dealership. Sweeping and vacuuming around cars that were well beyond my reach. Worlds colliding. Mendez's foundation cuts through that kind of bullshit. I lost a little money but I consider it one of those expensive cars that I never bought." She stood. "If there's nothing else?"

"We appreciate your time, Dr. Tam. I hope the rumors surrounding Elizabeth are merely such and we won't need your expertise." Roger shook her hand.

I followed suit. "Thank you, Doctor. Your story was inspiring. I wish I could read that kind of tale in the Herald."

"I'm neither unusual nor special, Mr. Farina, but I thank you."

"THOUGHTS?" ROGER ASKED when we were outside.

"I have another suspect or more to tag the Mendez attack. I'm not sure I've eliminated Elizabeth for you. What do you think?"

"Dr. Tam would be a difficult expert witness for either side. Elizabeth met the requirements for her release but without a thorough re-evaluation, I can't eliminate her capacity to do harm."

"We need more time for thought, though time isn't a luxury. What about my villains?"

"I dug up their past. Your instinct was right. They're thugs. Buddy Tkachuk's been inside twice for assault. Steve Rokon served with him in Soledad for drug possession with intent to traffic."

"Buddy could be on the hook for a third strike if my charge held up?"

"He wouldn't do twenty-five but his sentence could be doubled."

"He'd have motivation to lie but he hasn't pushed the charge against me, it was Rokon. Are they that close?"

"Look for another motive and another motivator."

It took me a few moments. "Buddy could roll over on the dentist rather than face double-time. Rokon's under orders."

"He's also a patient of Dr. Wharton."

"How the hell did you unearth that tidbit? Rokon swapping dental work for dirty work?"

"Could be. My agent talked to one of Wharton's ex-hygienists. She didn't like some of the job perks. She being a proposed perk on Wharton's side."

"Any luck tracing Buddy's hospital bill payments further up the ladder from Rokon to Wharton?"

"No. We'd need a legal charge to try to subpoena his bank records."

"I'd rather just phone or visit him and bluff him off. Does Buddy have any family? I could threaten to turn them loose on the contractor which landed him in hospital."

"There's an estranged sister. She lives in Oregon with her husband and two kids. The husband's a Baptist preacher."

"I can sense the reason for estrangement. How many times can you forgive the black sheep when his choice is not to ask?"

"No details given. A phone slammed in anger put an exclamation mark to the severed relationship."

"Without Buddy conscious to charge me, does Rokon's accusation hold any water? Legally?"

"Pretty weak. Your word against an ex-con on behalf of another ex-con whose looking at a long stretch if you can prove he was the aggressor."

"I'm partially relieved. I've no doubt Wharton's behind Rokon's alleged version."

"A likely scenario. Can I do anything more?"

"No. I need to continue my current case before retreating to the last. I'm on my way to Farina-Black."

"I heard about the auction excitement. We were overnighting on the boat and didn't feel the tremors. First I knew about it was a tsunami alert on the radio."

I left him and drove to Pops. After a ten-minute wait, Milt Canyon found me. He looked haggard.

"Geez," I said. "It's only Monday and you look rattled. Everything okay?" He'd been at the auction but missed the valet service Sunday morning.

He ushered me into his office. A picture of his wife rested behind his chair. His degree and various certificates surrounded his head like an aura when he sat. "Still unnerved, I guess. Sharon's on meds. She wants to move away from the coast. She has family in Phoenix. I'm not ready to give up my position here so, impasse."

"I'm sorry, Milt. Talk to Pops, maybe he can grant a sabbatical. Try out the desert for a few months. Sometimes family looks closer the further away they are. When you end up on top of each other, the lustre fades."

He nodded and shuffled papers on his desk. It was OCD-like as he moved them around, then resorted them back to their initial state. "Thanks, I might. Though funds are tight at the moment, not sure I could afford the time off."

"Isn't it all done by computers anyway?"

"Farina-Black prides itself on personal contact with our clients."

"So, you fly back and forth. Or send Sharon out for a few months. Let her try it out, then make your decision."

"Not your problem but I appreciate your suggestions. Here's the second list you wanted, investment firms associated with Mendez. As much as I could glean on a first pass."

Milt passed me half a dozen sheets. Six management companies who'd invested with Mendez. Six who'd lost their clients' money.

Milt's sheets gave the firms' names but also the portfolio managers who'd made the calls. His comments were written in pen, no electronic trail, and for my eyes only.

"It appears you know most of them," I said, scanning his comments.

"Four personally, the other two by reputation or through a mutual connection."

"Your comments seem fair on each. Risk taken on behalf of risk-friendly investors. Could've been any number of promising but ultimate failures. No one ruined or unemployed due to Mendez?"

"Two of the managers have moved on to other firms but that's not unusual in our business."

Milt's hand shook as he separated those two.

"Take it easy, Milt. Maybe you need to take the day off. I'm serious, go for a walk along the harbor."

"I'm good. I need to find a task to take my mind from Sharon. There's a major refit to perform for one of our pension funds."

I gathered the papers and slipped them in my blazer. "Thanks for this. Do you want me to say anything to Pops?"

"No."

His answer was quick. I wanted to see Pops regardless, get his take on the firms and the managers. But I'd keep Milt's troubles to myself.

I shook his hand and left him to his bigger task.

Pops had a minute to review Milt's data and hand-written additions. "What's your impression?"

"Nothing strong here. Losses and sour investments are part of the venture, especially if the client is young and can afford to take the occasional flyer. They can earn back what they lose. Not so easy for the mature investor, they want capital preservation first, mild return second."

Pops smiled approval. "You weren't a total washout in finance, were you?"

"I absorb," I said.

He pushed the papers back. "I also meant your impression of Milt. I'm worried about him. He's distracted. I put it down to troubles between he and Sharon but I can't get through to him."

I decided my commitment to keep out of it had been pre-empted by Pops' divination. I told Pops about Sharon's anxiety from Saturday's tremor and wish to move her and Milt to Phoenix. I also relayed my suggestions regarding a test-run or sabbatical.

"That might be something. I can set Milt up with a sister firm in Arizona. Thanks for the insight. Gives me room to manoeuvre him to a better state of mind." He jotted a note. "What's your next step?"

I patted Milt's information. "Tally this and see if there's any cross-over with some names I already have posted."

"The peripheral corkboard."

"You got it. What did you think of Marsh's column in the Herald today?"

"Nothing Mendez can scream libel over. I thought it was less harsh than it should've been. But we'll take care of our own kitchen, if we can."

"Speaking of, I had a visit from Percy Oaks with the Securities Commission, warning me off Mendez. I guess he didn't talk to Diaz or Marsh. Should I be worried about this guy?"

"When I said 'we', I meant our competition in the private sector. We'll steer our clients clear of anything smelling like Mendez in the future." Pops' intensity ratcheted up. He was ready to preach. "The Commission won't do anything in a timely fashion. If they had, Mendez would've been shut down a few years ago. They have the teeth but not the appetite. Oaks is making motions to look like he's earning his paycheck. When and if Mendez's suits come to trial, the only ones who'll look as bad as him will be the Commission."

"If they've the teeth, why don't they pressure Mendez to capitulate and make good what he can, without a hearing's publicity?"

"Oaks may be trying. Ask him if he threatens you again."

"I have his card. I'll phone him if or when my curiosity is too strong. I've other pursuits more enticing than talking with him again."

I TALLIED THE LIST on my way home. I was tired of harassment from Dr. Wharton, using Steve Rokon. I didn't want to go any further with Oaks. And I had too many suspects for Elizabeth's frame and Mendez's shooting.

The peripheral clue wall grew from Milt's list. I had two approaches, Elizabeth and Mendez's cases were related, though not as direct as her anonymous accuser proposed. Or they were unrelated. Who had it in for Elizabeth Rudge?

Her ex-husband, his second wife or person unknown. Jolene had seen enough of me for the time-being. I hunted down Jolene's brother Lawrence in Denver.

Someone picked up on the third ring. "Hello."

"May I speak to Lawrence Rudge, please?"

"Who's calling?"

If it was him, why not just say so? Game in play. My serve. "My name is Clay Farina. I'm calling from Pacific Grove on behalf of his mother. Elizabeth. If this is Lawrence, I'd appreciate a few minutes of your time."

"Is mom okay?"

Sounded like genuine concern, a good start.

"She's fine. I work for her investment firm and some recent allegations have upset her. I'm trying to make the allegations go away. When's the last time you spoke with her?"

"Let me catch up here, Clay. I've been in Canada the last two weeks. This is about that article on the real estate guy, right?"

Canada. Checkable if he flew or stayed in a hotel. "Oscar Mendez, exactly right. Do you know him?"

"I know his kid. Or used to. We ran across each other through high school. Not a full chip off his dad's block. Got the bent ethics but none of the old man's drive or smarts."

"The son have anything against you or your family?"

"That's an odd question. This Farina-Black, are they the ones who told my father to invest with Mendez?"

"No one at Farina-Black advised such shaky investment to any of its clients." Not as far as Pops knew. And he knew pretty much everything going on under its banner. "I ask the question for the main reason I called you. I'm looking for someone who doesn't like your mother. Someone who'd put this allegation to the police and the press to cause her stress, guilt and public humiliation. Since you offered up your opinion of Oscar Jr.'s questionable character, I thought I'd start with him. So, a grudge?"

"Naw. We got along okay; he was just another rich kid who liked fast cars. At least he raced on the track, not on the street, like too many of them."

One for Junior. "Okay, if not him, let's expand the circle. Anyone else dislike your mother enough to try this on? We start close in, then expand the set."

"You want me to say Tiffany, don't you?"

"Only if you think she's a possible."

"Well, she certainly trash-talks my mother in front of me whenever she gets the chance. One reason I don't keep in close touch with my dad."

"How does your dad feel towards your mother?"

"Guilt, I think. Lying in the hospital after he was shot, he was contrite. Too little, too late. The trauma of their marriage affected Jolene and I growing up. We both sought therapy after the shooting and during the trial. It helped me to know it wasn't my fault. I don't know if Jolene reached the same normal state. She buries herself in her work."

"I appreciate your candor. We'll move on from your dad and step-mother. Anyone else? Anyone who might want to hurt you or Jolene by working on your mother?"

"Jolene has had a few romantic partners since the folks' divorce. Nothing permanent, her business is her true love. Any other relationship runs a distant second. I suspect they all were relieved to move on."

"Do you recall any names?"

"No."

"What about you. Anyone you piss off capable of building this kind of retaliation? Personal, business?"

"I've seen a few lifetimes' worth of confrontation growing up; I avoid conflict."

He seemed genuine. Without body language, I couldn't be completely convinced but his reaction to a bitter family life rang true. "Here's my number, Lawrence. If you think of anyone or anything, even going back to the trial, I'd appreciate a call. I'm really trying to make this thing disappear for your mother. Unfortunately, I have to dig into it before I can make it vanish."

"Like Jacob Marley, right? We forge these chains during our life. I'm not saying my mother deserves this refresher course in public shame, but she didn't help Jolene or me by sticking it out and creating a daily battleground for us to witness."

"You have my sympathy. This can't be easy for you to be so objective about your parents."

"Never easy but it no longer brings up the old emotions. The distance helps."

"Enjoy the winter."

"I've become a snow junkie, so I will."

"'Bye." He'd already hung up.

I unpinned his card from the wall and filled it in. I was hesitant to give him motive for shooting Mendez so I dotted his card pink. I hesitated on yellow. Was he still traumatized enough to frame Elizabeth? I dotted that color too. Maybe he still harbored resentment against his mother. Strong enough to implicate her? Unknown. The tidbit he'd known Oscar Jr. might or might not be significant.

I surveyed the wall and tried various connections. Too early, they wouldn't come yet. I needed a break.

A visit to Steve Rokon would release steam. I'd try the Can-Am, then The Silver Sardine.

Chapter 19

The Can-Am motel was a washout. Rokon had left an hour before, according to the sharp-eyed day manager. I drove past the NorCal Bank but no Rokon there either. Unless he'd grown a conscience, he wouldn't be at the hospital so I headed for lunch.

The Sardine was cracking windows when I got there. I took a window booth where I could watch the front door and settled in with the Herald and California fresh orange juice. "And keep 'em coming." I instructed the server.

A group of three riders pulled into the lot. Back packs and stuff sacks were bungeed to seats and tanks. Minimalist tourers. Two wore pudding basin helmets and the third sported only goggles, doo rag and a hefty beard. I wondered which held more bugs. They consulted the sky, looked at the chalkboard 'Specials' sign, and entered, unfastening leathers and head coverings.

They were in a good mood and started with cokes. Perfect meat for Rokon, if he showed.

Twenty minutes later, the bikers prepared to dig into burgers the size of their heads. Rokon came in, slowed as he walked past them, then moved to the bar. I wondered if he'd walked or had other stopping places unknown to me. Maybe he had gone to visit Buddy.

He approached their table, mumbled something, then sat down in the fourth chair at their invitation. I could hear him start his spiel.

"I envy you guys. I ate tarmac a week ago. Bike's a write-off. Just waiting for my mate to heal, then we're out of here."

The chatter continued. The trio were roofers from Seattle, heading for Playa Del Carmen for the winter.

Rokon told his story, much the way Chevonne had outlined the other day. He showed the healing road rash on his arm and they bought him another beer. I kept my cool and waited him out. The trio finished their lunch. I left money on my table and slid outside.

I admired the bikes from a reasonable, unsuspicious distance. "Sweet rides," I said when the first got close.

"Thanks." The response was automatic, neither friendly nor 'who the hell are you?'.

"I overheard your plans; I wasn't snooping. Do you make the Mexico trip every year?"

He nodded. "We tried Arizona once. And Texas. Mexico's cheaper to live and we can work for cash down there as needed. Do you ride?"

"I do. Not at your epic level. I'm a day tripper. As a matter of fact, I'm the beaten rider in your new friend's tale. I saw him go down and high-side his pillion. We weren't racing. I slowed and tried to warn him about the frost on the road."

I made eye contact with the all of them. "Can I ask a favor?"

"Depends."

We weren't all chums yet. My side of the story wasn't worth a free drink.

"There's some dispute over what happened. Your pal inside has one story for beer and a different one on a police report. The second one is false but doesn't make me look good. If I needed corroboration about the version he just told you, can I have a name and phone?"

"Why would we do that?"

Helmets and gloves were being donned and legs thrown over saddles. I didn't have much time to convince them.

"'Cause he's a prick and his passenger is in serious condition. Serious enough that for the moment he's no use to me or the cops. All it costs you is a piece of paper. I'm not asking you to corroborate my story. I'm asking you to confirm his."

The spokesman reached inside his jacket and pulled out a card. 'Mike's Eave and Roofing'. "I don't know about the passenger but you're right about one thing." He let go of the card. "That guy is a prick."

"Thanks, Mike. I hope the cops don't need you. If they do, it'll be a local Sheriff named Dennis Levi. He's okay. Buenos Dias."

I tucked the card in my wallet and went back inside. Rokon had his back to the window. He'd missed my play? No matter, I'd bring him up to speed.

I sat, leaving one empty stool between us. I studied his face in the mirror. "Draw one," I said to the bartender, pointing at my selected tap.

Rokon tapped his bottle on the bar to signal another. He caught my reflection and passed by, then he returned, squinted and looked sideways at my profile.

"Do I know you?"

I faced him. "No, you don't know me at all. I'm the loser in your wonderful stories."

"Huh?"

"I'm the guy you tried to crash. I'm the guy you targeted with a false police report." I took a sip, not letting my eyes leave him. "I'm the guy you outrace every day in this bar to anyone who'll listen."

"Farina," he said.

"Your employer's bane. Or conscience. Antagonist. So glad you recognize me. I suggest you memorize my face, then take your buddy Buddy and go back to San Luis Obispo. Tell Wharton he paid the price he deserved and to continue to harass me through people like you is only going to cost him more. He's already footing hefty hospital bills, how'd he like a false accusation lawsuit against you?" The last part was bullshit; Rokon's allegations hadn't cost me material harm, but I was gambling he wouldn't know that.

"You're crazy. I never heard of Wharton."

"He's your dentist, Steve. You can also tell him I'm in touch with Buddy's family and I will tell them who hired him for the task which landed him in hospital. Wharton'll be liable for that, too." That might be bullshit as well, but I was pissed at all three of them.

Rokon laughed but there was little heart to it. "Get lost, Farina. You don't scare me."

"Like I didn't scare you on the highway. What did that misjudgment cost you? Your bike, your pal's health and you're stuck in a shitbox motel covering Wharton's ass for him. I'm not here to scare you, Steve. I'm trying to educate you. Get out and away from Wharton as fast as you can." I passed a ten to the bartender. "For his next two." I left my half full glass unfinished. "Is your life half full or half empty right now, Steve?"

I left, keeping my ears tuned for sign of movement behind me. You never know how hard to push before a guy will crack and resort to violence. I got to my car unmolested. Rokon's teeth had been pulled.

It felt good to unlimber my frustrations but it wasn't a fair battle. Rokon was in a corner, he just didn't realize it yet. Except now he knew my car, if he didn't before. Would he fold without one final go at me?

I decided to visit Dennis and bring him up to speed. I entered the station just as he was coming out.

"That was quick," he said. "I just left you a message."

"I've got some news for you, too." I reached for my wallet to give him Mike's card and the Rokon story.

"Mine's more important."

I didn't like the sound of it.

He grabbed my arm and steered us toward a squad car. "Where are we going?"

"Hospital. Buddy Tkachuk died an hour ago."

Shit.

Chapter 20

I related my encounter with Rokon while Dennis drove.

"I'll talk with him and up the priority on the investigation." He turned to face me when we stopped for a light. "I haven't pushed it because I know you wouldn't have acted as alleged. I'd like to see him charged with careless driving causing death. But my personal opinion only counts for so much. A complaint against you has been filed and the investigation must be completed. Waiting for Buddy's recovery is no longer an excuse."

"I get it, Dennis. Anything from the road scene help? I took some pics as well."

"I'll start putting it together. Let's see if Buddy said anything before he died."

We located nurse Figuaredo and the attending doctor who tried to revive Buddy. The doctor read the list of causes.

"Internal injuries, specifically massive kidney and liver failure. Mr. Tkachuk wasn't a healthy man before the accident. Needle tracks on both arms indicate heavy heroin use. We'll perform a post-mortem toxicology analysis. I suspect heroin wasn't his only choice of abuse."

I turned to Betsy. "I'm trying not to be insensitive here but did he say anything about the accident before he passed?"

She shook her head. "Last time he spoke in my presence was when you were here last week."

"What about his sponsor, Steve Rokon?"

"We left a message at his motel. I haven't seen him since Thursday or Friday. Mr. Tkachuk wasn't my only patient. We don't keep a visitor log. "

"But no one can walk into ICU unmolested?"

"In theory, no, but we get busy, Mr. Farina."

"Have you notified Buddy's next of kin?" I asked.

"We have nothing on file," said Betsy.

"I can help." I wrote out the information I had on the sister in Oregon. "They were estranged but sometimes a death can shatter the walls."

Dennis said, "I'll need a copy of the death certificate and the autopsy report. Thank you both."

"My thanks as well," I added.

Outside, we both took a moment to breathe fresh, unmedicinal air.

"Damn," I said, breaking the silence. "If they hadn't been chasing me, he would be alive. His death shouldn't be on my conscience but it is."

"Clay, he put himself in the wrong place at the wrong time, nothing to do with you."

"I won't let myself off so easy but I'm telling Pops I'm through with divorce work."

"Come on, I'll give you a lift back to the station. Not to be insensitive but you might consider filing a countersuit against Rokon."

"On what grounds? I wasn't hurt."

"Not physically. This development could be considered traumatic."

"I'll think about it," I said. Dennis was right, it could be for my own protection. I still had limited proof and it was my word against a heel and a dead man.

Our route took us near the County Herald's office. A small crowd stood on the sidewalk, peering inside.

Dennis swung into the curb and parked at a forty-five-degree angle. I heard loud voices as I followed him into the building.

IT WAS NOT WHAT I EXPECTED to see. Nor who. Junior Mendez was causing the ruckus.

Felicia Diaz was holding her own when we entered. Mendez was in a rage, verbally.

"You had no right to slander our family." He had sunglasses in his hands. "I'll show you how this makes me feel." He twisted them into a knot, then dropped them to the floor and crushed the remains under his foot.

"It's not slander, it's truth. On record. We printed nothing against your family, just the facts on your father's business." Diaz took a sheet of paper from her desk. "This is how mad I am." She crumpled and tore it.

I tried not to laugh.

Dennis stepped between the pair, standing sideways. I was glad it was him and not me. I didn't trust either of them not to escalate now that they'd each drawn a line in the sand. Or sand box. I thought of two kids in a playground, both wanting to scrap but unsure how.

A car screeched outside. I looked to see Oscar Sr. leap out of his Bentley and dash toward the door.

"Here comes another one, Dennis."

Senior Mendez saw Dennis. He gave me a glance then grabbed his son's collar.

"This is not how we act." He had to reach up to Junior's greater height but Senior's larger and lower center of gravity gave him the advantage. Oscar Jr.'s feet almost dangled off the floor.

"Okay, okay." Junior didn't struggle but his face was still angry crimson.

"Now that we're all calmed down." Dennis gave Felicia a warning look. "Let's discuss the future relationships here." He pointed to the Mendez's. "Please sit, both of you. Felicia the same."

I took a position on the other side of Oscar Sr.

Dennis kicked the sunglass detritus toward us, then stood in a neutral location, taking no side.

"Oscar," Dennis spoke to Junior. "I can't allow people to attack our journalist and editor every time the Herald prints an article someone doesn't like. There's no slander here, I've read it twice."

"Does freedom of the press include dredging up old rumors? My dad was shot, for Christ's sake. Why don't these so-called journalists dig into who instead of why?"

Felicia spoke. "If you wait for the Wednesday and Friday installments, you'll get some satisfaction."

"I'd consider locking your front door those days," said Dennis. "Not that I expect any more action from Mr. Mendez, but who knows who else is out there with a grudge."

"It's the risk we take and bear. I consider the Herald to be a responsible newspaper." Felicia's tone was now professional, her anger dimmed.

Junior snorted and Senior slapped his hand on a desk. "I have withstood allegations in print and in civil court. None proven. I have lost, and made, money for my investors. It's the risk I take and bear. Failure does not bring in more investors. If you think failure is my intent, then you are wrong. My son made a grave error today. I apologize."

Felicia said, "I have no intention of pressing charges. But keep him away from this office."

"Can you guarantee that?" Dennis stared at Junior.

The young man glanced at his father, then Dennis. "Yes."

Senior nudged him.

"Yes, sir."

"See that you do."

I held the door for father and son. Oscar Jr. walked away quickly.

"Be home for supper," his dad called.

I said, "Mr. Mendez, I'm sorry about your fundraiser going sideways on Saturday."

"You're Glen's son."

"Right. Clay." I nodded my head toward the Herald office. "I might have acted in poor judgment to protect my father in a similar circumstance. I can't fault your son's emotion, just the actual response."

"He has anger issues, I'm afraid. Not a good trait in my business. Or any business for that matter."

"What is his business?"

"He destroys race cars."

He was honest about that. I laughed. "Not much long-term future in that, is there?"

"I keep threatening to cease my indulgence but haven't. I keep hoping there'll be one crash which scares the shit out of him."

"Not my experience with racers. Failure without death can reinforce rather than stop the dangerous behavior." I admired his car. "How did you react to today's article?"

"I used it to start the morning fire."

"Did you read last week's articles? The ones on the Rudge family."

He nodded, now less friendly. His evaluation had changed focus from friendly stranger to what?

"Do you think Elizabeth Rudge shot you?"

"I have no idea. She shot her husband so the will is there. Why she'd come after me in obvious premeditation seems a stretch."

"Her ex-husband's divorce settlement included his investments with your companies. A portfolio which turned out to be a lot less than she'd counted on."

He opened his door and leaned on it. "I'd ask her, if you really want to know. Why do you care about her or me?"

"She is a client of my father's. The allegation of her involvement with your attack is stressful for her. I work for my father on the investigation side, aiding his clients to eliminate their difficulties if I can. Part of that process in this case, to prove she didn't do it, is to find out who did."

"You have my support. Whoever shot at me is still out there. And the police don't seem to give me priority."

"Can I talk further with you. This week?"

He looked at the ground for a moment, then me. Acceptance clicked for whatever reason. "Come out to the house. Wednesday after lunch. Do you know where we live?"

"I can find it. Thanks, Mr. Mendez."

He got in and smoothed away in a car worth more than my condo. Well, I thought, I had more room and a bathroom.

MY ADRENALINE RESPONSE had been tested twice today. Third time lucky, I thought, and headed for the Can-Am Motel to see if Steve Rokon had heard the news about Buddy.

I bypassed the office and went straight to room 12. I could see the open door from the lot below. A cleaning cart was parked in front of the next room. I thought what the hell, door's open, I'm looking for an acquaintance. I rapped on the door. "Steve?"

A woman in an apron wearing rubber gloves came out of the bathroom.

"Hi," I said. "Is your guest around?" I did a quick survey. There were no clothes in the open. The bed had been stripped but not remade. A pile of used towels lay on the floor outside the bath.

"He is gone. A friend?"

I took a chance. "Not really. He's owes me money."

She picked up the towels. "Not here. Check with office, maybe they have your money but I doubt it."

"Skipped?"

She shrugged and moved past me with the towels.

I peered in the bathroom. He was gone all right. I descended the weather-beaten stairs and entered the office. The vacancy in room 12 was confirmed by the manager.

"I gave him a phone message from the hospital," said Frecia. "Twenty minutes later, I saw him jump into a car with a shopping bag. Thought he might be stealing pillows so I went up to the room. Pillows were there, his stuff wasn't. He paid cash up to tomorrow. Then I would've asked for another week in advance. If he's your friend, tell him he's got a free day."

"Was it the usual cab company?"

"Uh, no. It was one of those ride-share rigs. I saw the card on the dash as they left."

"Could I use your phone?" I called The Silver Sardine? He wasn't there.

I called the hospital and spoke to the accounting department again. Buddy Tkachuk's last invoice hadn't been paid.

MY NEXT STOP WAS THE vehicle lock-up. I wanted to view what remained of Rokon's bike. The attendant had no contact info other than the Can-Am Motel.

"It's a write-off but someone'll buy it for parts. Motor might be salvageable," he said.

I raised an eyebrow. "Really."

"Buck a cc."

I did the math. "A grand seems a bit high for an unknown conditioned engine."

"You'd be surprised. Cheap for a race bike back-up. You interested?"

"Can I look at it?"

"Third row, half way down on your left."

The bright blue paint didn't look too bad on one side. The other side had no paint, very little bodywork and the remains of a mirror. The front end hung on to the rest of the bike by wiring and cables.

I took a few pictures while I replayed the scene yet again. I thought about the fading skid mark I'd seen Friday. I had one piece of proof which supported my story. I hoped an accident reconstructionist would see the evidence my way.

Chapter 21

It was mid-afternoon when I entered The Bay Grill. I phoned Ynez to ask her to join me but had to leave a message. Fine, I planned on pitting in for the foreseeable future. Dinner would be for one or for two. I wasn't moving soon. My conscience was not in the clear. A guy had died because of my actions. Not my direct fault but fallout.

Jonas raised his glass and I slid into the booth. "I'll have what he's having, please Cassie."

"And when he refills too?" she asked.

"No, I can't keep up that pace. I'm hungry. Any appetizers you recommend today?"

"The clams are superb," Jonas said.

"So are the calamari rings," added Cassie.

"Clams *and* calamari it is," I said.

I turned to my booth and possible dinner companion. "Where were you during the quake and shake?"

Jonas rolled his neck muscles. "Driving back from Half Moon Bay visiting a friend. I was five miles from home when the car wobbled. Thought I'd blown a tire. *Run-flat, my ass*, I thought. I pulled into a lookout. While I was standing there, the second tremor rolled through and I realized how prescient we'd been last week. The Jag decided to overheat. I waited an hour then limped home. No visible damage to the city, so a good thing."

"Nature's warning salvo. Do you think Californians are natural selection candidates for mankind's evolution?"

"Yeah, eliminate whatever gene compels us to live in beauty."

"Worth the risk, I agree."

Cassie set my wine down. "Jonas?"

"Yes, another please." He emptied his existing glass. "And you?"

I related the auction up to the tremor interruption, subsequent rides home, and the early Sunday morning valet service initiated by Pops.

"You skipped over the most interesting part."

"Which would be?"

"Ynez. What's the scoop with you two?"

"We took a road trip Sunday to Salinas Valley and she made me dinner."

"Who made you dinner?" Cassie arrived with my clams and Jonas' carafe.

"New lady in our private eye's life," said Jonas. "A professor."

"About time," said Cassie. "Is she slumming or do her fellow profs not make the grade?"

"Thanks for the confidence vote. I can hold my own, thank you very much."

"I'm teasing. Now eat your clams before I bring the next dish."

"Help yourself," I said to Jonas.

"Well, maybe a couple more won't hurt. How's the investigation coming?"

"Lousy." I let the first clam slide in and down. Jonas was right, they were delectable. "I have no shortage of suspects for either case. Oh, and I may be charged with vehicular manslaughter."

Red wine almost came out his nose.

"Okay, that is a tremor. What the hell?"

"I am the target of a vengeful dentist."

"The worst kind."

"His hirelings tried to wreck me, decided to turn the tables with a claim I was the one who wrecked them. The allegation might have gone away except the one witness, the passenger, who seemed on my side, died this morning. His partner has split, which may be a blessing. But I still need to straighten out the dentist."

"It sounds like his investment in revenge mounts daily. I say wait him out. Act at the nodal points."

"*The Art of War.*" It made sense on a rational basis but I hated waiting. My nature was to push through to resolution. Damn the nodal points.

"Waiting could be my only option. At least until I can make sense from the data surrounding the active case. What does Sun Tzu have to say about a multitude of potential enemies?"

"Hmmm. Nothing specific but if I was to adapt strategies for your situation it would be eliminate all you can, move ahead on the remainder one step at a time until your position is solidified."

"What if I just start shooting? Metaphorically. Pushing buttons." But in which direction? Something had to come to me first. Maybe it had and I didn't recognize it. More time at the peripheral wall? No, had to be in the field. I needed to make a few calls.

"Too random," said Jonas. "The feedback could be misleading for any number of unknown reasons."

I gulped the last clam in time for the next platter. "My wine seems to have evaporated, Cassie."

"I'm done my shift but I'll pass it on. Marv's on duty."

"Join us?" Jonas asked.

"Not for wine but I'll rest my legs before heading home. Dennis has a couple more hours to go."

"Then have wine on me and so can Dennis if he can join the party."

"I don't think he will. Surf's up and he's got me a new board to try."

Jonas snorted. He regarded the ocean as something to look at, admire and not engage. 'I don't like to be in water where I can't see the bottom,' he'd confided to me when we were teens and I tried surfing. I didn't suffer any deep-water anxiety; I just wasn't any good.

My calamari appeared with my second wine. "Thanks Marv."

Cassie showed up five minutes later in a sundress. Bikini straps over the shoulders revealed the swim suit ready for wetsuit coverage. She slid in beside me.

"I take it your case is proving difficult?" she asked.

"You could say that. And my non-case is worse. Did you ever run across the Rudges? Or Oscar Mendez? Junior or Senior?"

"I went to public school. Three mile walk uphill and into the wind. No parent chauffer or car when I hit sixteen. Saving my money for college."

"How's that going?" asked Jonas.

"Not bad, I'm doing online courses through Cal-State."

"Small beach," I said. "You know my mom teaches math there."

Cassie smiled. "No math for me. Environmental Studies is my goal."

"Do you know Ynez Jones?"

"I have her for introductory climatology. She's great. How do you know her?"

"Uh, she's the lady who made me dinner."

"No breakfast?"

"No breakfast."

"Whoa," said Jonas. "Slow down, he just met her."

I vacuumed the remaining squid rings and went to the bar. I phoned Elizabeth Rudge and arranged to meet mid-morning on Tuesday at her townhouse. Wednesday was Mendez Sr. I wondered how I could corner Junior. When he cooled down. Wednesday's column could start him off again.

I also wanted objective information on the new Mrs. Gordon Rudge but had no idea how to speak with her without going through Gordon or Jolene.

Dinner was somewhere between wine and scotch. Inebriation held no further insight for my investigation. I would need a different, sober muse. Rolling down the windows in the taxi freshened me up. I thought I could hike the stairs to my condo on all fours if I tried real hard.

The phone blinked its message beacon. Red, color of blood. I was still thinking about answering it when I passed out on the sofa.

Chapter 22

Tuesday morning crept in on little elephant feet. The blinking red light seemed to penetrate my eyelids. Conscience raised me to a sitting position and I debated whether the clams were coming back or staying put. When the initial queasies settled to a mild rumble, I tried standing. Hey look, mom, I'm walking. First destination, kitchen or bathroom? Last night memory. I chose the phone.

One message. Talk to me.

"Hi, Clay, it's Ynez. Monday afternoon. I know it's last minute but there's a faculty group heading to la Caliente in Carmel. We'll be there by five. If you can join us, that'd be great. Call me back or just show up, if you can. 'Bye."

The bathroom won the next stop.

Thirty minutes later, with bicarbonate settling my innards down to earthquake level, I tried Ynez.

"Hi, leave a message."

"It's Clay. Tuesday morning. I'm so sorry I didn't get back to you last night. I was exchanging case thoughts with a buddy and got home rather late. I'm out for the day but I'll call tonight." No need to tell her about the rough Monday morning that led to the afternoon and evening's choices. It was too early to start advertising flaws. She'd learn soon enough if we progressed further.

I transitioned to coffee and toast while staring at my board. Nothing came. I needed a different focus. Was I up to two wheels? Did I pass my self-proscribed limitations test? I judged yes. My concentration would be keener because it had to be.

Road gear on, I fired the Goldstar. The concentration zen required to ride well would aid my preparation to interview Elizabeth Rudge without her knowing she was being interrogated.

I found myself retracing Carmel Valley Road. Morning fog clung to the valley. The brisk temperature helped my recovery. Suitably chilled and fully woken, I took the turnoff to Laguna Seca. The climb out of the mist revealed glorious sunshine.

A few cars and bikes were wringing it out on the track. I parked beside the pit wall and listened to the whine of high-revving engines being tested and found up to the task.

"I thought I recognized the sound." Ed strolled up to me. "Want to run a few?"

I pulled off my gloves and helmet. "Do these eyes look like they can focus on entry and exit points?"

"I'm not an optometrist but I'd say keep it under thirty and stay out of the way. Why are you here?"

"Just going for a ride to clear the 'webs. I think it's working."

A yellow and black production racer screamed past in the wrong gear.

"Listen," said Ed.

The car disappeared from sight but the revs dropped.

"He let up," I said. "That's why he was in fourth gear instead of fifth, didn't want to downshift. But he'd be passed in a race by every driver keeping their foot in it."

"It's your pal, Mendez." Ed put a finger to his lips for silence. We heard a rev spurt, then the previous whine of an engine pushed beyond its redline. "He missed the upshift. Chances are he'll pit and get the mechanic to work on the linkage."

"Between his brain and feet?"

Ed laughed. He pointed to a guy sitting in a lawn chair reading a magazine. "That's his crew, if you want to wait with him." Ed looked at my bike closer. "Your bike looks ready. Tape the lights and I'll let you go."

"Not today, thanks anyway." I pulled the key and moved over to Mendez's one-man pit crew.

I crouched down to his eye level. "He'll be coming in?" I asked.

"Who?"

"Mendez. Aren't you wrenching for him?"

He put down his magazine. "That your BSA?"

I nodded.

"Sweet ride. You must know British John."

"My bike put two of his kids through university." An exaggeration but John had guided me through the restoration and continued to monitor me and the BSA to ensure I didn't abuse or not use it.

The guy held out his hand. "I'm Rob. Mendez is an idiot. Unless you're a friend. In that case, he's a rich idiot."

"I've heard. He pays well?" Had Mendez Sr. passed on the contractor lesson?

"He does. Not always on time, bit of a game with him, I think. Still, this is better than pounding nails on some building project or working in a truck stop."

The buzz of the production racer's approach cut short the rest of our conversation.

Mendez left it running and climbed out. He lifted his visor. "Linkage," he yelled. He pointed inside the car. "See what you think."

Rob held his hand out for Mendez's helmet. He wadded it on and belted into the driver's seat. He accelerated smoothly from the pits and changed gears at the maximum torque point until I couldn't hear him anymore.

Mendez finally noticed, and recognized me. "What the hell are you doing here?"

"Coincidence," I said. "I was out for a detox cruise and stopped here. I'm glad you have an alternate physical mechanism to unwind your emotions. You were right to take offense on behalf of your dad, but not by threatening Diaz. I think your dad can look after himself."

"Yeah, he can but I don't often get the chance to prove to him that I'll be ready on the day he can't."

He glanced at my bike. "Does that thing race?"

"Better than I do. I reach my limits before it does."

"That's the book on my talent as well."

Candid, I thought. Knows his reputation. "At least you're out here practising to improve."

He snorted. "I'm not sure. I might have to try a different class. Try my skills against the weekenders. Maybe these extra laps will give me an edge over them."

"How did your dad really take the article? There'll be another one tomorrow. Do you have cause for concern?"

"It isn't your business, is it?"

"I'm meeting him tomorrow to discuss Elizabeth Rudge and their potential link."

His lips tightened and his hands clenched. "You're as bad as that paper, dredging this crap up."

"I'm trying to find out who really shot your dad. Isn't that what you want?"

He relaxed. "What I want is to move past it all."

Dropping down a few notches in the racing game because Mendez Sr. couldn't afford to fund his son in expensive cars?

"Then what better way to end it for good? Tell me what you think. Tell me who you suspect?"

"You're not a cop."

"No, I'm not. But I am actively working the case. You've had months to think about this. You might have thought of something you haven't told the police. Some piece that might not have looked like evidence but now does."

Rob trundled back in and parked the car under its pit tent. Mendez and I walked over. Rob's feet stuck out the door sill and I heard a ratchet click. He cursed, ratcheted again and crawled out. He held out his hand. "Bushings are worn. It was sloppy in first and second."

Not for him when he left the pits and not for the higher gears that Mendez was botching. I kept quiet while Rob fished in his gear for replacements. He disappeared under the car for two minutes and three expletives. My kind of mechanic. He slid out. "Try it now."

Mendez climbed in and fiddled with the shifter. He turned to me. "Why don't you get your bike. We'll do a couple of laps together. Maybe I'll think of something on the track that will help you."

Or try to crash me for the second time in a week. The first didn't work out for the aggressor but that was bike versus bike. Cars always win versus bikes. If it was the only way I could get him to open up, then so be it. Hangover or not. I guess I was going to spin a lap or two.

"Give me a few minutes to prep." I picked up a roll of tape from Rob's tool chest. "Can I use this?"

Rob smiled. "No problem."

Mendez buckled in.

Rob whispered, "The tape'll go onto Mendez's shop supplies bill. By the way, he lifts for the crest between turn one and two and before the rise at the corkscrew. If you feel like passing."

"Thanks." I wheeled the bike over and taped mirrors, headlight and taillight.

British John had installed safety wires for the critical fasteners, 'in case you want to try something stupid on the race track'.

I thought it looked 'the business' in John's vernacular and left it. Sidewalk racer, that's me.

I LET MENDEZ LEAD FROM the pit, glancing over my right shoulder to gauge the other cars on the track. The first lap warmed my tires and I learned Oscar's preferred cornering line. I noted how soon he braked. I was also trying to decide if I should let him win or try to beat him. He might be an average driver but he'd know if I wasn't trying.

He upped his speed along the main straight before turn one. He let up over the rise before turn two as I'd heard and Rob had informed me. I could have passed him then but it was too soon and I was running a pace I wasn't certain I could maintain for a full lap or two. We diced through the course and he let up early before the quick left-right of the corkscrew. He took an odd line through turn eleven exiting to the front straightaway.

As we neared the pits, Oscar stuck his left hand out his window and made a circle. One more lap. I'd get him on that final turn if I could keep up.

I had to twist throttle insanely to keep Oscar in sight. I got on his bumper when he lost speed at the corkscrew and stayed with him going downhill through turn ten. I readied for my move as we picked our line through turn eleven. Oscar took his wide choice and I gripped throttle. I twisted it back, not forward, using my engine's compression to slow. His rear swept across my line as he changed course. If I'd accelerated, we'd have occupied the same space at the same time. Déjà vu from the previous Monday. In this scenario, a bike loses the anti-physics overlay with a car.

He pulled to the side and exited the main circuit. I idled into the pits, shut off and leaned the bike on its stand. My hangover had gone.

I peeled the safety tape to keep my shaking hands occupied while I thought of a few words.

Oscar tugged his gloves off coming toward me. "I thought you had me on the last turn. Wheel slipped and I almost went off. You ride well." Mendez seemed to harbor no ill will. I guess he saved it for his on-track personality.

"I didn't know we were racing," I said. I balled the last of the tape and tossed it in a trash barrel. "Did you think of anything?"

He shook his head. "Not a thing."

I'd been suckered.

"See you around, Farina." He swung a leg over my bike and grabbed the bars. "If you ever want to sell this, let me know."

"I don't think that will happen." I put my gloves back on and signaled his time on the seat was done.

I waved to Ed on my way from the paddock. He just shook his head. Mendez hadn't made a complete fool out of me; I'd done that myself. I'd learned something about him, though, and maybe it had been worth the judgment lapse. Oscar Jr. wasn't a bad driver; he was an angry driver and that was worse. His non-racing personality had been reasonable but now I'd seen him in full temper twice. Once at the Herald's office and now here. He was volatile. Was he a planner or dangerously impulsive?

I tried to shift my thoughts to Elizabeth Rudge on the ride home. It didn't take; neither had the morning's shower. I'd need another before I visited her.

'I'D SHOWERED, CHANGED to professional going-to-meetin' clothes and piloted the sedate Beetle to Palm Estates.

My head refused to release the replays of my ill-conceived on-track dice with Oscar the younger as I parked in Elizabeth's drive. My strategy with the first Mrs. Rudge would be no strategy. Let Elizabeth direct the conversation until I gained more insight or inspiration.

The interior of her townhouse glittered. Glass display cabinets filled with crystal figurines, a huge chandelier and triple French doors leading to a glass-rooved conservatory prismed the sunlight everywhere.

Pictures of Jolene and I assumed Lawrence, he bore a faint resemblance to Gordon, decorated the walls and mantle. From infants to adults, their pictorial story was documented. Love or guilt? Maybe both. A large one of the three of them in tropical gear, Gordon obviously cut off one side, stood on a desk. A balcony, ocean and what I thought was Diamond Head in the background. A handwritten note across the side read 'Thanks to Norm and Rose, Liz'.

"Tea and cake?" she offered. "I made the cake this morning. I hope you like it." Elizabeth was dressed in a silk kimono and silver slippers. Hair coiffed and makeup applied lightly but elegantly. She, like her home, was on display. I didn't flatter myself that it was only for me. This was how she lived. Her social circle might be smaller than it was during her and Gordon's high times but it didn't mean she'd given up trying.

I tried the cake while my tea cooled. "This is delicious. When can I move in?"

"Hah. You might not care for the lettuce and ham sandwich I had for supper last night."

This didn't look like a sandwich household but I grinned anyway. "I can't remember what I had for supper last night but a sandwich would've been a better choice." And not drowning it in alcohol.

"How are you progressing, Mr. Farina?"

"Clay, please. I'm not old enough to drive a Buick or be called 'mister.'" I babbled while trying to form my strategy on the fly. Best to be straight up. Trust her? Until she tried to perforate me with .22's.

I began. "I've discovered that Oscar Mendez Sr. is not a popular man, though many people appear to support his charitable causes. Behind the smiles and handshakes seethe distrust."

Elizabeth picked up her saucer and cup. "Yesterday's article in the Herald stoked the fire, just as last week's columns paraded my shame in case anyone wasn't paying attention five years ago."

"The immediate response came from his son. Oscar Jr. showed up at the Herald's office in full berserker mode."

"Oh, dear. Did he do damage?"

"Only to a pair of expensive sunglasses. I was with the cop who was first on scene to settle him down. His father showed up soon after. I challenged myself in the moment that I might've reacted similarly if it was my Pops under negative scrutiny."

Elizabeth's gaze went to the nearest photo of Jolene and Lawrence. Did she regret Lawrence's absence as a protector?

"Your daughter confronted me last week. Asked me to not add my contribution to the Herald's fire by asking questions."

She didn't change expression. "I'm not surprised. She thinks I'm vulnerable. Three years in prison eradicated that trait, trust me, Clay."

Once more, trust. Okay, in this minor claim. "I thought you and I should talk about who might want to cause you 'inconvenience' via the letters to Colin Marsh and the police." Let her start it before I provided a nudge.

She shook her head. "I don't know. Gordon's friends?"

I waited but she'd reached a blank.

"Tiffany?" I suggested.

"I said 'friends', not overlord. Tiffany has won. She got him. Her only resentment toward me should be that I made him available."

"No financial grudge on her part?"

She thought about it. "They live on a yacht. Before she married him, she lived in a coach house in Pismo Beach. I know, I had the photographs of Gordon's car in the driveway. She could be a suspect, though I'm not sure she's smart enough."

"What about him?"

"Gordon? Smart enough not to. If Jolene or Lawrence discovered he'd wrote the letters, their split affections for their parents would evaporate. I'd have their undivided affection."

It was time to expand the circle. "What about former cell mates? Prison guards? Anyone inside you might have cross-threaded?"

She raised an eyebrow.

I rattled off further explanation. "Cross-threaded. Conflicted. Ticked off."

"Aha. I was a model prisoner. I continue to help parolees seek legitimate employment. I volunteer at the outreach center. I've never had a nasty encounter, in or out of jail."

"No resentment. You were from a different background than most of your fellow inmates. True?"

"Oh yes. But the nature of my crime elevated me, or lowered me, to a popular level. I'd done what many of them wished they had. Shot the abusive partner."

"Hang your picture in the cellblock?"

I didn't get a smile. She seemed more introspective than amused.

"Metaphorically, perhaps they did."

Move on from suspects to here, while she focussed internally? "Okay, your enemies remain hidden. If you had to testify about your feelings toward Mendez, what would you say?"

Her knuckles tightened on her teacup for a moment. She forced herself back in the chair. "I transferred some anger from Gordon to him during the settlement but what would more money have brought? It wouldn't change what I did to Gordon. I'd have a bigger house, maybe. Drive a Caddy instead of a Buick." She held up her hand. "Relax, I am old enough to drive one." She set her cup down. "A matter of degree, Clay, not substance. I have accepted who I was and who I am now. I try not to miss things. But I do miss some people, no thanks to Gordon."

"If they're so shallow, then are they worth missing?"

"Thank you. Sometimes they are. I'm still dealing with that."

"I admire your honesty. Too many in your situation would claim they don't and that they're better for it." I had one more piece of cake.

"I'm sorry I'm not able to help more, Clay."

"Me too. I will keep digging. Find out who really shot Mendez." I finished my tea and stood. The extra cake weight was already building thigh muscle. Good choice on the second slice.

"Please call again."

"I will return for my Christmas shopping." Let Dennis, Jonas and Pops chew on Samuel's ties and support a good guy. "I'd prefer you didn't tell Jolene about my visit. She has a full load keeping that stable running, she doesn't need an excuse to pay me another visit."

"I love my girl. She doesn't circle around; she heads for the core."

"She obviously loves you too." I resisted the temptation to take more cake for the road and jogged ten paces to the Beetle.

Elizabeth had done more than prepare a cake, she'd prepared herself. The self-control mantra gleaned from her psych sessions had been well learned. With the one exception, the comment on the loss of certain friends, she'd presented the veneer of a mature ex-debutante, rehabilitated ex-con and altruist.

Had I missed anything else? If so, I'd taken enough interest in her words, body language and surroundings to tickle the subconscious into an 'aha' moment at a suitable time.

I SCRIBBLED NOTES WHEN I got home. I'd gone from a bad decision to race and a blurred visit to my client. Both provided minor character insight into Mendez Jr. and Elizabeth which I documented. I left unwritten the insight into myself.

Could I change the day's fortune to the good side of the coin? Worth a shot. I tried Ynez again. My luck was improving, she answered on the second ring.

"Hi, it's Clay. Any faculty soiree tonight? I am available."

"Not tonight. Our systems crashed and I've a bunch of online learners I need to reconnect to my webcast."

"Is it difficult?"

"No, utterly boring and time-consuming."

I would not be easily daunted. "Can I pick up dinner and oversee the buttons being pushed and clicked?"

"I'd love it. Wine corks make the best key pushers."

"Understood. Would fish and chips be satisfactory? Or am I breaking a professional ecology commitment with seafood?"

"I gotta eat. Very acceptable. I know my limitations and withholding meat protein is not one."

"I'll see you in an hour."

I phoned the Grill and put in my pick-up order. I showered and changed for the third time today. Third time lucky.

Ynez had her table set and I dished out while she fussed with her laptop. "I swear I should take out a marriage contract with the internet," she said.

"I call for a temporary separation. Dinner is ready." I carried a glass of wine to her desk.

We clinked and sipped. She took a deeper draught. "It goes well with my cider vinegar for the fries." She closed the Cal State page and we retired to the table.

The screen displayed a trio in straw sombreros and swimsuits, bathed in bright sunshine. "Your screensaver," I said. "Family? You're younger. Looks warm wherever."

"Yeah, me and the folks. Our last family trip to Cancun. Not warm, hot. I lose myself in the scene on blustery days here."

"It's the second such vacation snap I've seen today. Elizabeth Rudge had a Hawaiian memory displayed prominently."

"We migrated south rather than west. My uncle bought a timeshare in Cancun and let us share it while I was growing up. After dad lost his business. It was a nice winter break from the weather and the stress. I miss it."

"Why did you give it up?" I sprinkled vinegar and salt on the huge-cut fries.

"Oh my, this fish melts on the tongue." She took a second bite before answering. "I got too busy pursuing my doctorate. Mom and dad tried a couple of cruises and got hooked. I didn't want to take over my uncle's commitment when he tired of it. With school term demands, I can't get away except in peak family vacation times when everyone else hits the air. Usually, by the time I'd surface from writing or marking final papers, anything I could afford was booked. I've had many Christmas 'staycations.'"

What happened to the Rudge's vacation spot? I'd ask Pops if he knew. Or Jolene if he didn't.

Ynez forked in more fries. I realized I'd been fingering mine. Subtly, I changed to cutlery. "You kind of know about my day fighting with electrons. How was yours?"

"This morning I took a few laps at the raceway, cleared the cobwebs from Monday evening's poor judgment in my wine tolerance." I held up my hand. "Don't ask, I'm not ready to reveal all my flaws yet. This afternoon, I spoke with Elizabeth Rudge in her massively over-decorated home. But she serves great dessert."

"I might have a few cookies stashed in my freezer."

"My sweet tooth has been sated for the month, thank you."

We finished our meal over small talk about the university.

"I know one of your online learners. Cassie Levi."

Ynez's brow creased. "Really? How?"

"She's working her way through university serving where this delightful meal came from. The Bay Grill. And her husband, Dennis, is the sheriff investigating Rudge's and Mendez's cases."

The crease smoothed. No rival. I was flattered. I also could have completely misread the situation.

Ynez's computer sounded a guitar chord. Her eyes flicked to it but she didn't move.

"You have marvellous self-control," I said.

"I'm enjoying the meal and your company. Why would I interrupt it for the electronic leash?"

I offered a second glass of wine. "Exactly how I feel most of the time. My methods and life are low-tech."

"Let's move to the couch." She stood. "I will finish this glass and then return to my duties."

"I'll clean up while you work, then slip into the night."

"Thank you." The breeze had cooled and Ynez closed her patio door to a sliver. "What are your plans tomorrow?"

"Read Colin Marsh's column when the Herald hits the streets and see if it jogs any neurons for my investigation. Then I will visit Oscar Sr. in the afternoon. Get his pulse on the person who attacked him, see if he has any notion about why someone would finger Elizabeth Rudge for the attack. Observe his precautions so it won't happen again."

"Sounds more exciting than my day. Though this weekend I'm leading a field trip into Los Padres. The national forest. Do a pre-winter undergrowth evaluation."

There went any plans I had for us. "Do tell." I hoped my fake enthusiasm wasn't too obvious.

Ynez thankfully didn't tune in or diplomatically chose to ignore my small disappointment and dove full on into describing her research tasks for the students.

We finished our second wine helpings and I took care of the kitchen duties while Ynez re-connected to the internet world. When I'd put the last dish away, I returned to her desk.

She looked up. "Four more assignments to go through. Sorry, this isn't exactly romantic but I really appreciate you making the effort with dinner and all."

I bent down and kissed her cheek. She turned and offered her mouth. It was warm, firm and too brief. "There is no rush," I said. "I'm confident we'll have time before the next 'quake to take further steps."

"Thanks for understanding, Clay. I do want to spend time with you."

"Me too. Damn life gets in the way. I leave you to yours and I retreat to my sanctum sanctorum and noodle the day's progress, if any." And exorcise road rage demons before they invaded my dreams.

Ynez saw me to her door and we kissed again. This time, anything but brief.

I SCANNED MY CORKBOARD, adding sticky note thoughts here and there. 'Vacation Property?' was the last to go up, between Gordon's and Elizabeth's cards.

I stretched out in my easy chair and considered what I learned today. Two people with disguised personalities. Oscar Jr.'s ruthless on-track persona and his under-control off-track one. But he'd shown the blood anger one off the track at the Herald office. The social mask was the disguise?

Elizabeth was much more in control of her angry persona. She'd reconciled with Gordon's incompatibility, according to her and Dr. Tam. Had she transferred the hate to Mendez? Why not? If he'd indirectly taken away her lifestyle, her social circle and her prestige. Couldn't she decide he was the direct cause?

Tiffany Rudge could harbor the same resentment, perhaps toward both of them. Gordon? His resentment was on display. His quick flash of anger about his living quarters hadn't been hidden. He'd shown no regret at letting fly.

Jolene? It was a stretch to think she'd turn from mother-protector to hater. She worked hard but for her passion. Lawrence? The son was an unknown. He'd run away from the daily conflict of choosing between parents. Would he meddle remotely? I didn't get that sense from our phone conversation.

Other investors? They were taking the legal route, though chances were slim they'd recoup more than honor. I broke the category down further to individual versus institutional investors. Guys like Armand Moore were the hardest hit and he accepted his own contribution to the financial downfall. Was he really that honest with himself?

An institutional involvement was still an individual choice. One or two or a handful of portfolio managers made the decision to sink clientele money into Mendez's schemes. They had a duty to diligently research his offerings. Someone hadn't. I looked at the short list Milt provided. Who got exposed? Who got fired?

The last two cards I looked at directly were two outliers. Dennis Levi and Colin Marsh. The recipients of Elizabeth's secret accuser's tipoff.

I closed my eyes and concentrated on the newsman. Where was Colin Marsh when Oscar Jr. showed up? Had they received other feedback, less violent, on the previous week's thread? Had Marsh lost money? My limited knowledge around small center print media types was that reporters and editors didn't get rich plying their trade. That was for the owners. If Marsh had a retirement egg, had he been daring enough to throw it into Mendez's frypan? Did he write the accusation himself, hoping to nudge progress?

Now that was an outlier. I opened my eyes and stared again. Too early to dismiss it. It was worth a chat with Marsh to find out about responses to the Elizabeth profile series. Maybe he'd provide information on his journalism methods I could adopt.

Chapter 23

I called Colin Marsh early Wednesday morning and arranged to meet at ten. It gave me time for a sidewalk breakfast and perusal of the latest column. Firecracker stuff for certain regulatory quarters.

The Herald's lights were on but the front door was locked when I arrived. Monday's intrusion by Oscar Jr. had altered their security. I knocked and waited. Marsh's head popped above a cubicle wall and he waved. The door buzzed and I went in.

"Have you heard from a Percy Oaks?" I asked. This week's second article focused on the history of failures by the state Security Commission to protect neither the public nor the legitimate brokers.

Marsh ushered me into his half-walled cubby-hole. "Yeah, he phoned Monday afternoon, telling me my articles were interfering with the Commission's Mendez investigation and encouraged me to stop. I didn't have much more on Mendez so I said I was done with his specific operations. Oaks' indignation gave me more than enough inspiration for today's piece."

"You got him right where I wished I could," I said. "He appears to be a sanctimonious turd who won't allow anyone else to do his job, when his effort is piss-poor. Even printed his own custom business cards, not government issue, I'm sure."

I pointed to the door. "I'm relieved you opted to prevent another Oscar Jr. type incident, especially when Diaz is here on her own."

"Yeah, I should've taken the bullet on that one, so to speak."

I didn't share his grin. "I wouldn't tempt fate with those terms. I wanted to ask about other feedback you've had, from Elizabeth's series as well."

"Comments are posted on-line, anyone can read or post a follow-up within our guidelines. I haven't refused any."

"I'll go through them if you can spare me a terminal. Can you give me the gist?"

"Elizabeth's supporters outnumber detractors by a wide margin. Mendez's support is weak."

"Any similarity in any of the comments to your original tip?"

Marsh paused. "Good question. I didn't notice an obvious comparable."

"Can I have a copy to look at while I go through comments?"

"Sure." He moused and clicked for a minute, then the printer above his desk whirred and spit it out. "Let me set you up next door."

I followed him to another cubicle and watched him log in to the paper's site.

"I've set each installment in a separate tab." He left the tip note.

"Thanks."

I began with the tip note. *Mendez and Gordon Rudge shot with similar gun. Coincidence or habit? Check Mrs. Rudge's loss thanks to Mendez. Maybe she isn't cured.*

Then I reread last Monday's article before digging into the comments. Part one solicited mostly sympathy or disinterest. 'Old news…Paparazzi trash…Lifestyles of the former rich and infamous'.

Wednesday's response was more of the same but Friday's brought out a couple of rants questioning why people like Mendez lived the high life while their victims suffered. One said if Elizabeth had pulled the trigger, she was a hero. I held up the tip-off note to study the syntax for similarities. Nope. The two spelling mistakes in the new comment were my clue.

This Monday's comments were mostly conspiracy theories about pyramid schemes conceived by the Illuminati, the IRS or various churches. Today's article had only two comments thus far, both decrying the Securities Commission's lack of action on specific cases, which to me looked tenuous at best.

I read the tip note again. Succinct, grammatically correct. Something any high school graduate should be capable of writing. Or a journalist. Or a newspaper editor.

Maybe Oscar Jr. had it right, increase circulation under the guise of investigative journalism. Where did legitimate news end and sensationalism begin?

I HAD TIME TO SPARE before meeting Mendez. It was Wednesday. Jolene Rudge's errand day. Samuel would be on his own at the ranch. I decided I needed a new tie.

J & L Stables' parking lot was empty when I pulled in. I couldn't see any sign of Jolene. I listened for activity while I walked around the fences. A few horses neighed and I returned the greeting.

I heard the scrape of a shovel inside one of the buildings and entered. The haze inside smelled of feed and manure. Or money.

"Samuel?" I called.

His head popped over a half door. "Closed this morning, mister." His head dropped from sight. More shovelling.

"I'm not an equestrian today, sir. I desire a Tie by Samuel. I was here on the weekend and my friend so admired your neckwear, I thought it might help my chances with the lady."

He popped up, a smile creasing his weathered, friendly face. "Really? I remember you now. That's a mighty pretty lady you brought. She was very nice to me."

He exited, wiped his hands and moved toward the door. "Follow me."

We tracked across an outside show ring, he greeted the horses one by one. They responded with nuzzles while I watched my step.

Samuel's digs comprised a trailer of unknown vintage, colorfully painted in blue, red and yellow, and masked from general view by a cedar hedgerow.

I removed my shoes at the steps and climbed inside. It was far neater than I'd imagined and put my housecleaning efforts to shame. "Sit," he commanded.

He stood in the doorway to his bedroom and the rear of the trailer and lifted the hinged bed board. He returned to the table with a box. The selection overwhelmed me. I'd thought of getting something cowboyish for Halloween but I could not refuse a garish plaid atop the pile. It would be a hit at the Farina-Black Christmas party.

I made a show of examining all of them, just to be friendly. "Ms. Rudge around today?" I narrowed it down to three.

"Nope. Wednesday's business day."

"It's between these, Samuel. What do you think?"

He held them up one at a time against my neck. "Don't know. They'd all do."

"You folks ever have trouble with wild critters coming in and raiding the food. Raccoons, coyotes and the like?" I made a fuss over the plaid, got up and checked it in the bathroom mirror.

"Sometimes. I don't like to interfere with any of nature's creatures but the horses come first."

I sat down, the plaid tie affixed to my shirt and a silly grin on my face. "This is the one, isn't it?"

"It was meant for you. Should I wrap it?"

"Absolutely."

He dug in a drawer and returned to the table with some previously-enjoyed birthday wrap and twine.

"How do you deal with the animal pests. Traps, firearms, poison?"

Samuel stopped his wrapping. "I couldn't shoot anything. Poison's too dangerous and traps are just cruel."

"Ms. Rudge handles the problem, then?"

He nodded and finished wrapping.

"Is she a good shot?"

"I don't like to say. Hard for me to watch, you know?"

"I know, Samuel. I know." I felt like a shit. This was a kind, gentle soul, working his heart out for a woman I was trying to incriminate.

"How much do I owe you?"

"I don't know. I haven't sold any before."

"A good tie in a store can run forty or fifty bucks," I said. "Something as unique as yours has to be in the range."

He looked shocked. "I thought ten would be too much."

I passed him twenty. Any more and he might talk to his boss about the crazy spendthrift. "If you keep this between us, Samuel, I'll be back in a month or two to purchase a few more for Christmas presents. I don't want anyone to steal my thunder by getting to you first. Okay?" I offered my hand.

"It'll be our secret. You're okay with me mail ordering some, when I get my website?"

"Absolutely. I expect mine will be an excellent investment."

I carried my prize back to the car, wondering if he would tell Jolene about my visit. I wasn't too worried, if she was involved criminally, it might shake her up enough to do something stupid.

I still felt like a shit.

MENDEZ'S GATE OPENED after I identified myself and smiled at the camera. The drive was short. A willow copse hid the house from the cul-de-sac turnaround. Mendez beckoned from a carport. I got out and followed him to the rear.

The mansion was smaller than I expected; they'd saved the space for the back yard. He and his wife didn't need to join a country club, they had it all here. Pool, tennis court, flower gardens, all bordered by Sinai cedars. I noted security cameras mounted on the eaves.

"Thank you again for seeing me, Mr. Mendez. I realize this isn't an easy time for you."

He was dressed in a plantation owner's white suit. We sat under a patio umbrella so he didn't need a wide-brimmed boss hat. "It is the curse of success, always someone trying to tear you down."

"Or take you down. Have the latest news pieces brought forth any threats?"

"Not to me."

"You have increased security?" I pointed to a nearby camera.

"We put those in after the attack. Now that we have it, it doesn't seem like we need it."

A maid appeared with a jug of iced tea and glasses. She poured two. "Thank you, Esmeralda."

I offered my thanks and sipped.

"What can I do for you, Mr. Farina."

"Well, I'm trying to get Elizabeth Rudge out from any suspicion that she is connected to your attack."

"The story or tip that the Herald printed seems more like vengeance against her than me."

Mendez wasn't stupid. He'd shrugged off threats and notoriety before but he did analyse them. "You may be correct. Or it may be a subtle way of getting at you. Or even both of you. Do you know her?"

"I knew her ex-husband, before their notorious incident. We had occasion to encounter the Rudges socially and Gordon invested in one of our properties in Santa Cruz."

He loosened his jacket and crossed his legs. I noticed he wasn't wearing socks. The idiosyncrasies of the rich.

"After that, I didn't see them anymore. I think Gordon lives up the coast and I don't see Elizabeth at all."

"He's in Santa Cruz, living on a boat with the second Mrs. Rudge. Elizabeth's townhouse is in Monterey. Palm Estates."

"I know it. My father owned the land it's on at one time."

"Is it your development?"

"No. He levered the land into a larger deal in Salinas."

"I've heard a bit about your dad. He was a visionary."

"He worked hard, saved hard, lived frugally and wore himself out."

I stared to the back of Mendez's kingdom. "Without being able to enjoy his legacy?"

"He enjoyed the toil more than anything. He may have died before it was fair but he left nothing undone." Mendez smiled. "I'm enjoying it for both of us."

"Do you work as hard as he did?"

"I have to. Despite being second generation American, I'm still a Mexican in the eyes and minds of most investors outside California and many within."

Maybe he did work hard. A family trait. His son worked hard at being a dick. "I too often forget my privileged existence," I said. "My folks worked hard too to be where they are. But I appreciate the difference. They never had to overcome prejudice. Do you think racism was behind your attack?" Not the smoothest segue but it was all I had besides straight out asking 'who dunnit?'.

His thick eyebrows rose and his lips parted. "You're the only one who's asked that. Everyone, including the police, assume a disgruntled investor was trying to make a point. Not to kill me, but to vent anger, throw a scare into me. Force me to reimburse all those who lined up to take the risk I offered. Which I cautioned them about. Real estate has occasional setbacks. Saturday night's earth tremor dropped property value in a dozen or more venues. The state as a whole saw billions of dollars of potential investment evaporate."

"Isn't that old news, though? We have tremors all the time."

He shook his head as if I had asked why the ocean was wet.

"That's just one lurking disaster which makes secondary capital seek more secure, more stable places. Raging brush fires do the same."

"People rebuild."

"Instinctively, not rationally. Sometimes investment is the same." He touched his fist to his chest, then his temple. "They follow emotion, not reason."

I could see the issue in a broad sense. Too many people without alternatives in where to live. The disasters weren't the cause of the panic, they were a constant. Population expanding into more fragile environs was the root cause. I wondered what Ynez's opinion was. "Panic sell-offs in the stock market."

"My business doesn't always follow stock trends but the variance can be just as dramatic."

"And just as traumatic to the individual. When they have everything tied up in one spot."

"I don't tell investors to risk all, that is a decision they make for themselves."

I took in the house and grounds in a sweeping look. "You've obviously diversified enough to suffer setbacks." Though, according to Pops and others, Mendez had profited from his clients' losses as well as their gains.

"I keep faith. Long term vision. That's what drove my father."

"What drives your son?"

Mendez's mood changed. The smoothness evaporated from his voice and manner like the money he'd referred to. "Competition. The racetrack is his battleground. Risking physical harm for the adrenaline rush which comes from every small victory." Mendez leaned forward. "My son may not win many races but the skirmishes won in every corner and straight I can understand. I hope he can transfer the experience and passion to the family business."

It was clear he understood the similarities. It was also clear his support continued only due to paternal indulgence. "My dad had the same hope for me once. The family business. I don't possess the required aptitude." Or the temperament to be responsible for clients' futures.

"You work with him, though. That alone must give him satisfaction."

"Sometimes. Aggravation as well. Before I go, can I ask if you've had any threats or unusual messages, encounters and such since Monday's *Herald*?"

"No one's shot out my porch lights or graffitied our gate. My office hasn't suffered any disturbances."

"Phone calls? Hang-ups? Text messages?" Jar his memory with specifics.

He shook his head. "I didn't like what they printed but I can't control the press. I'm not in the right circle for that."

Playing the discrimination card? I didn't think so. But he thought there were people who could control our local journalists. "Any names of those who could?"

He stared at me for a few moments before answering. "Forget I said that, I should be grateful to the *Herald*. Their negative publicity could work in my favor in a trial."

"Glass half-full?"

He shrugged and looked at his watch. I recognized its logo. Another Bentley. Yeah, this guy was riding a financial roller-coaster. Hardly.

"I have an appointment in Salinas, Mr. Farina."

I stood on cue and offered my hand. "I appreciate your time, Mr. Mendez. Call the police if there's fallout from the articles." You might be a crook in finery but the next attack might not be a warning.

"I will." He was already ushering me to the driveway along the side of the house.

I waved goodbye but he'd already turned away. I had been invited, met, engaged and filed away under 'Inconsequential'.

Chapter 24

I added two unnamed cards to the corkboard. Instead of names, I wrote categories. *The Herald influence. Mendez's Real Estate competitors.*

I considered their significance while I prepared supper. Every time I tried to narrow my list, more possibilities arose. I felt like an Egyptologist in a sandstorm. With each stroke of the archeologist brush, more worthless dust buried the truth.

The peripheral evaluation didn't help. I sat on the balcony and toasted the sunset; for two hours until weariness overcame me. Weary of trying to force ideas which refused to manifest for the conscious mind. Tomorrow would reveal the next step or not.

In my dreams, the sandstorm was replaced by a flood. My evidence ditch filled with water each time I got to the bottom. I never got a long enough look to see what lay there.

The phone intruded Thursday morning before I was ready. I answered it anyway.

"Clay. Good morning."

"Pops."

"Did I wake you?"

"Stirred me from the twilight consciousness."

"Whatever the hell that means. Should I apologize?"

"No. I was waiting for inspiration which sometimes appears just before full alertness. What's up?"

"How's the case?"

"I have too many leads and too few ideas to proceed. I've talked to Elizabeth, her son and daughter, the ex, Mendez Sr. and Junior, Colin

Marsh and his editor, and one of Mendez's more visible victims. Oh, and you know about Percy Oaks. I miss anyone?"

"Sounds like you've covered the lot. What's next, a second round?"

"I don't know. I need more information to go back at them to make it worthwhile." I needed a change. Focus or venue? "Do you know the publisher of the Herald?"

"No." Pops paused. "I don't think it's anyone local. The Herald's part of a community paper chain. Most of the revenue comes from the weekend sale flyers in the Friday edition."

"Is circulation an issue?"

"It's integral to the business. The higher their circulation, the more they can charge to distribute the sales inserts."

"Do they syndicate any of the columns outside the group? The Mendez stories for instance?"

"You'd have to ask Diaz or Marsh." He sounded like I'd used up my three wishes.

"You're right, I should have asked them yesterday. Not a big deal but they could be doing this to Mendez and Elizabeth strictly for their own gain. The tip-off note to Dennis Levi and Colin could've originated with Marsh himself."

"That seems a stretch. Hard to prove."

"And pretty sleazy. I think it's too much of a risk to be probable, but when I get tired, my brain starts to dream up possible." I would change venue and focus today. Let my hindbrain noodle the Rudge case. "I need to pay Wharton a visit today. The road trip might trigger new ideas."

"Doctor Wharton? In San Luis Obispo? Why? I received Linda's second and final fund transfer yesterday. Case closed."

"Not for him. It's complicated, not worth reviewing over the phone. I'll fill you in later."

"Don't screw it up."

"Too late. He already has." I hung up.

One full breakfast later, I geared up and rolled the Goldstar from my garage to the sun-filled driveway. I performed the start-up routine with a mantra-like reverence. When you got it right, it started on one kick. Get it wrong and you wore out a knee. Today was a good day.

While the mechanical steed warmed up, I slipped on a backpack with water and snacks, fastened my helmet, dropped the visor and stretched on leather gloves. I idled away from the complex, keeping in mind some of my neighbors were likely still asleep and coasted downhill to the main road.

Today was not Laguna Seca. This was a gentleman's outing, albeit on one of the greatest British motorcycles ever conceived on one of California's great drives. I accelerated along the water and corrected, not just British, an all-world bike, if antiquated by modern standards. Those dimming empire engineers knew how to put the rider, mount and road together as one.

The miles rolled by with ease. Knowing the road made it more pleasurable as I could appreciate the changing fall colors. The concentration required for piloting and enjoying the surroundings were just what I needed. By the time I arrived in San Luis Obispo, I was barely able to work up a tizzy toward my nefarious dentist.

It had to be done and my peace of mind would return back on the coast highway heading home.

I rolled past Wharton's building, a two-storey Spanish art deco piece with law, chiropractic and accounting firms sharing the space. I drove to the rear parking lot. Wharton's Lexus convertible sat in his reserved stall. I knew his routine for lunchbreak at 1:30 and parked the bike in the shade far from the back door. I left the helmet, gloves and jacket with the bike and settled on a grass patch next to his car to have my lunch.

The building door opened and a couple emerged. Not Wharton. They chatted without attending to the strange biker eating his lunch in their lot. The man turned when Wharton came out. They all said 'hi'. Witnesses were good.

I stood up when the dentist got close. "Have you heard from Steve Rokon lately?" I asked.

He blinked, key fob in his hand. "I don't think I know him. What do you want now, Farina?"

"Good recovery, bad answer. Before he disappeared, did Rokon tell you Buddy Tkachuk died?"

"Steve, Buddy, where do you come up with these names?"

The couple watched us. "Same place you did. Steve was a patient. Buddy was the extra punk he hired to do your dirty work on me. Technically, Buddy died in your employ and due to your instructions. I'm sure his family, no matter how estranged, would be interested in that." I pointed to the other two people. "Either of them a lawyer? You might want to confer. In the meantime, stay out of my life. You screwed up yours and paid the penalty. Quit trying to compound the damage. You won't win. A man has lost his life. You had a part in that. Shut down your need for revenge against me. It's already bad, don't make it worse." I climaxed my oratory by finishing my sandwich in one gulp and waving to the onlookers.

Wharton noticed the slip of paper I slipped under his wiper blade.

I washed the sandwich down and explained. "Buddy's sister. You can contact her or I can. At least pay the last hospital bill. It won't reveal you. I'm sure the cops can trace Rokon's money trail back to you with what they have already."

He crumpled the paper but didn't throw it away.

I got on my bike. If he had a response, I couldn't hear it above the exhaust as I blipped going past him. His eyes were downcast, shoulders slumped, the paper still in one hand. He'd kept his cool in front of the other people, I'd know them if I had to call on them. Wharton's downcast posture indicated a man who was no further threat.

My spirits weren't lifted by the encounter. I'd threatened him. I was justified, his thugs had tried to hurt me. Being right isn't always a win. It felt dirty.

As anticipated, the return journey improved my mood. The final thirty miles flew past in a series of full-lean turns, hunched down acceleration bursts and inhaling the sea air. By the time I pulled into the Silver Sardine, my brain was calm. No clarity on the case but fresh. I parked beside two Texas cruisers.

I leaned on the bar, looking for the server I'd talked with before. "Coffee," I ordered.

I caught Chevonne's attention while she filled orders on her screen. When she'd finished scrolling her fingers on the tablet. I moved closer. "Hi, remember me? You filled me in on the great motorcycle racer-chaser guy. Steve."

"Yeah." Her smile was for a potential tipper, not Clay. I couldn't fault her for that.

"Have you seen him in the last two days?"

"No. It doesn't mean he hasn't been here. He could've come in after my shift."

"I think he had a routine." I passed her my card. "If he does show up, please give me a call."

She read the card. "Investigator. What are you investigating?"

"He owes me money."

"I can believe that. Was he a client?"

"Indirectly." I slid her a ten. "For my coffee."

"Thanks, Clay. If he shows up, you'll know."

I remoted my answering machine from the bar phone. I didn't want to miss a second Ynez message by half a day. No need to worry. No messages.

I needed a hot shower and scotch in the comfort of my nest to reclaim the calm of the ride and to plan tomorrow. The push back toward Wharton felt good and it accomplished my intent. What was the nodal point in Elizabeth's world? Mendez's?

SUNSET FROM MY BALCONY was fast and as always, magnificent. Writing pad in lap, I listed names down one side of the paper, places, timelines and miscellanea down the other.

Who or what to push? I ticked individuals and was left with the unknowns. I pulled out the list Milt had made for Pops and me. Institutional investment managers. How had they reacted to the Herald's Mendez rejuvenation? I phoned Milt's number to leave a message and was surprised when he answered.

"Milt, it's Clay. Does my dad know you're burning electricity at night?"

He laughed. "No, I'm reviewing the Phoenix clientele, in case I'm transferred."

"Is your wife anticipating the move?"

"She's already there."

He didn't sound as enthused about that situation.

"Can you spare me some time in the morning from your dual position? I wanted to go through the list you made in detail, if we could."

"Sure. Let's see, tomorrow's Friday..."

I heard rustling of paper. Unless he'd started a fire in his office. "How's ten-thirty?"

"Perfect. It'll give me a chance to digest the last installment of the Mendez chronicle in the Herald." And pop in to see if more angry readers had reactions.

"They still on that? I haven't had a chance to read the latest. You can fill me in."

"Will do. Thanks Milt, see you in the morning."

I called Ynez. "Hi, it's Clay. Can I treat you to dinner Saturday?"

"Thanks, field trip this weekend."

"Oh, right. I left my memory somewhere on the road between San Luis Obispo and here today. Lunch tomorrow? Breakfast? Unless I'm sounding too desperate by this stage."

"Not at all. I like desperate. But it will have to wait until next week. I've got a zillion things to prepare and pack. Releases to collect. How's the case? San Luis part of it?"

"No, that was closure for older work. Enjoy your field trip. Is that the right thing to say?"

"Yeah. It's good to get out of the classroom and into nature's laboratory. I want these kids to get used to practical science. I have to run but call me Monday. 'Bye, Clay."

She was right, the real work took place in the field. Not in offices or on corkboards, but in my profession, interviewing and evaluating. I'd run out of names to pursue. Maybe Milt could provide more leads.

Chapter 25

Colin Marsh's final column for the week focused on the enablers of scammers like Mendez. The institutions who didn't complete their due diligence in vetting potential investments for their clients.

The pressure to move quickly drove some wealth managers to proceed before they should. The mantras of 'long-term plan' and 'balanced portfolio' took a back seat to greed. The brokers in these fantastic deals charged front-end commissions to ensure their clients got in. They also assured clients the worst-case, high-risk losses, would be regained by the conservative portions in their overall strategy. Great, if you have decades to recoup.

Marsh wasn't swayed by any of it. He stopped short of collusion accusations but the implication was there.

Milt was late but I passed the time re-reading the article. I was three-quarters through when he came into the room. He saw the paper.

He tapped finger hard on the table and paper. "Sorry I'm late, I took the time to read Marsh's latest."

"Appropriate timing for our discussion, though."

Milt's voice intensified. "This kind of shit stains us all. I've had four clients call me this morning for reassurance. Bloody irresponsible." He sat, not looking at me.

I pulled out his list of institutions who had gone with Mendez. "Marsh wasn't wrong," I said. "I grant you his words could be irresponsible from your perspective. Pops probably feels the same."

"He does. We had a meeting first thing to settle on the Farina-Black position and communicate it. Your dad suggested we be pro-active to phone every client. I haven't had the chance. They've phoned me."

I went back to the list. "Who's soiled here. I won't repeat it outside this room but if you had your pick of those who had a vested, not necessarily illegal, interest in pushing Mendez's scheme, who would it be?"

"I thought of that when I assembled the list from public knowledge and private conversations with my colleagues outside Farina-Black. There's two." He stroked a fingernail under two companies. "Both small. This one's a three-person show. This one a solo effort but she uses some freelance agents. Not saying she's dirty but some of these freelancers make more from the seller than the buyer, if you understand."

"Yeah, I got the hint from Marsh's article. Any stronger and Mendez Jr. wouldn't be the only one showing up ready to vent at the Herald's office."

"Mendez Jr.? Explain."

I told Milt about Junior's rage toward Felicia Diaz following Monday's article on his father. "He was more pissed than his old man."

"Senior's bulletproof in more ways than one. If he had a low-boiling point, he'd be selling paint in a hardware store. The pressure would crush him if he couldn't take it in stride." Milt flushed. "Junior's too volatile from what I know and have seen. I wouldn't want to be raising him."

"I think he's raised as far as he'll get. You don't think he'll inherit the business?"

"If he does, it'll be its death knell. Oscar Sr., for all his flaws, is personable to the point of charisma. I've seen him work his charm in front of a hundred skeptical brokers."

"How does he do it? Physically he's a gnome."

"And he uses it to advantage. Every flaw, he turns into a positive. Self-deprecating and challenging, he encourages his audience to be the visionary he is, his father was. Makes them think his gift is transferable to those brave enough to follow. Then to lead." Milt's face returned to pink. He might not like Mendez but he envied the man's style.

"Anything else?" Milt asked.

"No. Thanks for the time."

"Thanks for the break." He'd calmed. "Back to the phones."

I singled out the one-woman investment house and gave Pops a buzz on the interoffice phone. "Pops. Milt's given me a couple of ideas about Mendez. Would Colleen Axford know me by sight? Or name? She's an independent investment advisor."

"You better come into my office. Now."

I trotted along with my list and notes. Inside his domain I asked, "You do know her?"

Pops looked mad. "I know her to say hello, that's it. No reason she'd know you other than by name. Are you going undercover?"

"Just a little fishing. I'll give her my first name and say I'm getting a feel for her services." He still looked mad. "What's bothering you?"

"I had a call from Linda Wharton this morning."

Uh oh. "Something's upset her?"

He jabbed a finger in my direction. "You. Her estranged husband called her last night and told her to keep her dogs off. Apparently, you threatened him yesterday."

"I warned him. He hired two guys to wreck me. One of them, Buddy Tkachuk, is dead. Buddy's fault, not mine. The driver, Steve Rokon, wants me charged with trying to wreck them. It could mean vehicular manslaughter. Rokon was Wharton's patient. I told the dear doctor to lay off and I thought the dead thug's family had every right to believe him liable for the death, since Buddy died in Wharton's employ. Wharton was paying the man's hospital bills through Rokon but I think the law could connect him. I'm sorry it blew back onto her. I was trying to close the man's vengeance against me."

"Well, sometimes, you have to take a little heat. Your priority is to protect the client. In this case, Linda. She's thinking of pulling her funds. My first interest is for her personally, the loss wouldn't hurt us materially in the short term, but our reputation would suffer in the long."

"You're right, Pops. I reacted poorly. Should I call Linda? Explain the circumstance?"

"Call and apologize, yes. Details and motivation, absolutely not. She doesn't need to know about our risks."

"Will do."

Pops pointed to his desk. "Use my phone, the number's on the writing pad. I'll leave you alone."

I sat and took a number of deep breaths myself before dialling. To my resurgent discomfort, she answered. No hiding behind a message. "Ms. Wharton? Linda, it's Clay Farina. I am so sorry my actions yesterday bounced back on you. I didn't anticipate the possible result and I should have."

"I was shaken, Mr. Farina. I know the separation will produce angry encounters but I don't need others causing them, James and I will fight each other with vigor and hate before the end."

"Understood. I poked the bear with a stick."

I got a chuckle. "From now on, the stick is mine alone."

"Again, understood and again, my deepest regret."

"Thank you for calling, Mr. Farina."

"If there's any more fallout, you phone me first, okay?"

"Okay."

I gave her my number and hung up. Tough lesson for trying to be a tough guy. I should have left Wharton alone and let the truth find its own way.

Pops wasn't in view when I left. I guess I would never be too old for a scolding, especially when I deserved it. I was glad I hadn't told him about my dice with Oscar Jr. on the race track. Another case of short-sighted reaction and poor anger management.

AXFORD AND COMPANY occupied a modest office on Marine Drive. An overhead bell tinkled with the door. A young man appeared through an inner door while I perused various brochures and quarterly reports.

"Hi, can I help you?"

"I'm collecting information." I held up Axford's latest summary. "I've come into an unexpected inheritance. A surprise gift if you will. It wasn't in my plans so I thought I might like to take a real flyer, you know?"

"You should really consider it part of your overall plan, not just a one-time deal."

"Is Ms. Axford available? Maybe she has some ideas." I didn't want to insult him but I wasn't looking for a freelancer or junior partner.

"Sorry, no. She's out of town on business." He reached into a drawer behind the reception table and pulled out an 11 by 17-inch piece of computer-generated art. "This might be more what you had in mind."

A grand rendering of a multi-phase, varied housing development surrounded by desert, golf courses, riding paths and adults riding custom golf carts along palm-treed lanes beckoned. "Arizona?" I asked.

"Yes. Axford and Co. will be the exclusive California agents. Investors will enjoy a first right of refusal on prime lots for their own eventual sunshine getaway. It's an existing property which stalled part-way through construction. All permits are still valid; environmental restrictions less than any development in California, and most importantly, quake-free. The original developers ran out of vision and funds. After last week's earth tremor, inland get-away or retirement property is looking pretty inviting. The new principal timed this rejuvenation perfectly." He retrieved the paper and laid it on the desk beside a plan.

"What sort of return are we talking?"

"I'm not authorized to specify but double-digits are our target."

"Have you got a brochure I can take with me?"

"I'm sorry, no. When Ms. Axford returns on Monday, I believe we'll be ready to drop. Can I ask your name?"

"I'll drop in Monday. Thanks."

I tinkled the bell on my way out. It looked like a Mendez clone. Buy cheap, maybe from yourself. Bring in a new cash-flood for show. If it succeeds, great, if it fails, you got your money from the second sucker round. Milt's tag on Axford was right.

I RESISTED GOING TO the hospital to determine Buddy's remains' final fate. My curiosity was fuelled by anger and I needed to change my attitude. Rationalizing that Buddy's death had been related to me was an excuse, not reality. He chose his lifestyle, whether or not he accepted the inherent risk had nothing to do with me. He could've easily harmed or killed an innocent victim. My involvement saved someone else's life.

It was all self-delusional bullshit, of course, and I knew it. I just couldn't figure out the real answer. Maybe I wouldn't be doing this when I finally grew up.

I added Colleen Axford to my corkboard, with a questionable link to Mendez. I also added cards for Pops, Milt and Roger Schopff. Since I had a bounty of suspects, a few more names wouldn't make a difference, not as suspects, but as catalysts for connections I hadn't made.

I found Armand Moore's card and looked him up. No phone listed. Beetle time.

He was still trimming bushes when I parked opposite his driveway. Or maybe he'd taken time off since my first visit and it was time to prune.

"Mr. Moore. Hi. Nothing slows nature, does it?"

He looked neither glad nor mad to see me. Today, I'd take that effect.

"I hope you don't mind me dropping by, I had a question or two."

He wiped his brow and returned to his task. It wasn't a no so I pressed on.

"I've met the infamous Mendez, and his son, for that matter. Senior has it under control, doesn't he?"

A shrug.

"Was his self-assurance why you invested? A personal trigger."

He stopped his work and took a few moments to consider. "It wasn't him at all. Not at first. I'd never met Mendez. I overheard a few guys talking at my golf club one afternoon. At least two of them were investment brokers, judging from their talk. I never got a good look at any of them. They were on the other side of a cedar hedge. One was espousing this great opportunity. 'Couldn't miss, great track record' and half a dozen other buzz phrases. I kept listening until I heard the name of the development and I called my manager from the locker room."

"You ever hear them again? And put a face to any?"

Moore shook his head and raised his garden tool. "Nope. I haven't been around the club for a while, dues were one of the things I trimmed." He snipped the shears shut on a wayward branch.

"What was the club?"

Moore pointed the shears north. "Two miles up the road. Sea Grass."

A new connection, if true. One for the board. The problem was without corroboration, Moore's story couldn't be verified. "I know it. My father's a member." Farina-Black couldn't be the only investment broker with a membership. Likely one of a dozen or more.

"Good for him."

Moore had sunk into not-glad-to-see-me mode. I couldn't blame him. I'd reminded him of one more thing he'd lost. "I'm sorry to dredge up bitter memories. I'll be moving on."

He found another stray branch to vent upon.

DENNIS WASN'T IN SO I left a message. "It's Clay. I need to catch up and lay out a scenario on Buddy's accident. I'll be at the Grill. If you get this in time, can you bring the accident scene photos? Thanks."

Jonas was deeply engrossed in his phone when I slid into his booth.

Cassie appeared before he disentangled himself from whatever information whirlpool had him trapped.

"I'll try one of your non-alcoholic beers, please."

"We have three." She listed names of major breweries' varietals.

"Which one gets the best reviews?"

"I couldn't say and I've never tried one."

"Okay, which one have customers ordered seconds?"

"The oh-point-five."

"That will be mine, thanks."

"Jonas, it's me. Earth."

He put down his phone and peered at me.

"That's one reason why my cell is five years out of date and sitting in my desk, uncharged," I said. "I'm too easily distracted as it is, I don't need another time-sink."

"The new *opiate of the masses*, my friend. There are kernels of gold in here." He tapped the screen.

"And acres of dross. I need a weekend distraction. Any suggestions?"

"Break up with your new lady already?"

"No, she's away on a field trip."

"There's a wine festival in Santa Rosa. You could be my designated driver."

Cassie presented my near-beer. I said, "Thanks. If Dennis comes in, I'd like to talk with him."

"Sure thing. Jonas?"

"I'm content, thank you."

I sipped. Hmmm. Hard to tell if the taste would improve, stay the same or deteriorate with each swallow. "A chance to haul around your inebriated body and soul. No thanks. Check your phone. Santa Cruz might be doing a Hot Rods on the Beach thing. That I will drive you to." I did not want to spoil a weekend sitting roadside while the auto-club tried to revive one of Jonas' vehicular prima-donnas.

Jonas suckled the electronic teat while I struggled with more of the non-beer.

"Tomorrow at noon. Food bank drive so all we need for admission is spam and soup."

"I'll pick you up at ten. There's a guy I want to talk to in the marina." Gordon's take on Mendez's charisma and my further take on Tiffany Rudge were in order.

Dennis' bulk dropped into a chair. "Anything else for you gentlemen?" Cassie asked.

I pushed my unemptied glass to her. "Bring me a real one, please. Pacifica Pale."

"Jonas, how are you?" Dennis asked.

"I thrive, thanks. Keeping the peace rolling?"

"Easy most of the time. Except for your friend here." He nudged me. Dennis wore a lot of hard gear. It was like being nudged by a sharp boulder.

"None of it my fault. I'm a bystander."

"You're a nexus," said Jonas.

"I agree, whatever that is," said Dennis.

"Well, enough about me," I said. "What's the latest on Steve and the late Buddy?"

Cassie delivered my beer and a water for her husband.

Dennis pulled out a notebook. "Steve Rokon picked up a wire transfer for one thousand dollars Monday morning at NorCal Savings & Loan. He returned to the Can-Am Motel, cleaned out his gear and hasn't been seen since. I called Buddy Tkachuk's sister in Redding on

Tuesday afternoon. Her reaction wasn't surprise. She asked what the plans were for Buddy's remains. I said it was up to her but the hospital would want his bill paid before releasing the body. She said that was typical Buddy and hung up."

"Is the body still there?"

"No. His bill was cleared this morning. Over the phone. Hospital didn't want to breach their privacy rules but when I said Buddy was part of an ongoing police investigation, they relented. A James Wharton."

I spit beer.

"You know him?"

"He's the guy who hired Steve and Buddy to wreck me. I spoke with him Thursday outside his office. I told him I thought Buddy's family might be interested to know who Buddy was working for when the accident occurred. I intimated he might have some liability there. Guess he did the right thing, once he cooled off."

"What do you mean?"

I explained my involvement with Wharton and his wife and his ongoing resentment. "He pushed me, I pushed him, he pushed the wife, she pushed Pops, Pops pushed me. I learned a lesson."

"Sounds like an ancient family sitcom," said Jonas. "Playground egos."

"You're not wrong," I said. "At least he paid Buddy's final dues. I didn't completely screw up." I wiped up the beer I'd snorted.

"Sometimes you gotta push," said Dennis.

"It's knowing when is the hard part," Jonas added.

"Where does this leave me with Rokon's accusations?"

Dennis ran his glass in a circle in the condensation on the table. "The only other witness is dead. A bottom-feeder criminal who owes money and has taken a runner. I'd say the case is in limbo."

"But not dead."

"No. I don't think you'll have to worry. Without Wharton to pay his bills here and risking a false accusation and defamation charge, I'd say it's over. I doubt I could get approval to waste time visiting him in so far from our jurisdiction."

"I'd like more assurance. Let's compare photos." I laid out my faint-tracked images. "I've showed you mine."

Dennis opened an envelope and took out Deputy Reiger's shots.

"This one," I said. "The skinny, single tire skid mark on the right side of the lane. It's mine. Rokon's bike has a much fatter footprint." I pointed to one shot of the wrecked bike, showing the rear tire's width. "I panicked, hit the rear brake lever without thinking."

"I see," said Dennis. "So?"

"So, my bike is British. Like most of its contemporaries, BSA never switched over from left-side foot brake and right-side shifter. I couldn't brake and kick at the same time with my left foot. Rokon and Buddy passed on my left. Rokon confirms that in his statement."

"Pretty convincing," said Jonas.

Dennis didn't speak but shuffled the pictures around.

"I can also supply the name of a waitress at Rokon's adopted bar while he was in town who'll repeat the story he related every night at the bar. A contrary version to his charge filed with you. I want this to be more than put to sleep, I want it closed and burned."

Dennis sighed, then nodded. "I'll talk to her and our reconstructionist when he's available. If it hangs together, I'll apply to have the complaint expunged."

"Now that's a cool word," said Jonas. "Onomatopoeic. Expungggggged."

Dennis laughed. "I'd use it more often with that reaction. Anything else?"

I asked, "Any new tips on Mendez? The articled in the Herald stir fresh responses?"

"The anonymous tipster hasn't followed up. Another dead end." Dennis drained his water and stood. "Keep out of trouble if you can, Farina. At least for the weekend."

"Jonas and I are off to Santa Cruz."

"Should I warn my counterparts?"

"Hot Rods and wine, how much trouble can we get into?" said Jonas.

"Lord save us. Maybe there'll be another 'quake." He gave Cassie a peck on the cheek on his way out.

"Make sure we're in a single storey motel in Santa Cruz," said Jonas.

"You got it."

Chapter 26

It was Saturday morning and the Beetle had delivered Jonas and me enthusiastically if not speedily to Santa Cruz. I followed a candy red, billeted 1932 Ford highboy along Beach Street. Where the hot rod turned, I turned. He hung a left toward the boardwalk. I thought, what the hell, and slipped under the advertising arch.

A guy in a white vest adorned with a blue ribbon approached holding a clipboard. "Did you pre-register?" he asked.

"We're audience," I said. "Looking to park."

He leaned on the door sill. "We're short on show vehicles. Your bug will amuse the old hippies. For twenty bucks you get two t-shirts, a mug and a dash plaque."

I passed him twenty and filled out the entry form.

More guys in vests waved us to a spot between a VW campervan and a BMW microcar. The 'odd rods' in their own corral.

"Do we have to stay here all day?" Jonas hung the t-shirt over his shoulders. He could fit in it twice.

"No, the car'll be safe. We'll look at the other rigs, then find a shady spot to have afternoon tea."

"Gimme the mug."

It was insulated and had a snap on top.

"I can fill this with wine. You have all the tea you want."

I lowered the top on the Beetle but rolled up the windows and locked it. "Let's stroll."

When you're in a show, you either let the world walk past you and miss out on the other cars or you check out the cars and avoid the opportunity to bullshit about your own. We'd come to see, the exhibitor opportunity equated to free parking. And free t-shirts. We didn't have lawn chairs to lounge in. We'd walk until we got tired enough to find seats at an outdoor grill or on the turf.

The crowd was thin, it wouldn't get busy until mid-afternoon, when the weekend's shopping was done.

"What do you want to see?" Jonas asked. "There's a lot more than hot rods. I see a line of Euro sports cars; good old American muscle starts over there." He pointed to a bright yellow Camaro parked sideways to us. "A Yenko, highly sought after if it's genuine."

"I've seen a few of these at Pebble Beach Concours over the years, including the hot rods." I saw Gordon and Tiffany Rudge stop at the Camaro, Gordon animatedly chatting with the guy getting out of the car. Tiffany looked everywhere but toward the car. "We're doing muscle cars. That's Gordon Rudge."

"Tally ho," said Jonas. "Are we surprised to run into him or are you targeting him?"

"I am surprised. I thought of dropping in for a chat at his yacht. This saves time."

As we got close, I could tell that Gordon was explaining more to the owner than the other way 'round. "It was white when I got it," he said. "Had the wrong wheels, wrong manifold. It had been drag-raced so a shitload of stuff had to be changed for the street. Took me four years to get it right."

"I bought it in Petaluma a year ago," said the owner.

"That'd be the man I sold it to. Glad you're keeping it on the road and not stored in a bag inside a hidden garage."

"You driving anything now?" The owner was polite. There was always someone who knew more about your car than you did at these shows. Or thought they did. Regardless, they were driven to share.

"No. Haven't found anything that cranks me up. Not like this did." Gordon looked at the car with love in his eyes.

Tiffany didn't look at it at all.

"Mr. Rudge, hi." I sidled in.

His expression was neutral. "What brings you back to our town?"

I pointed vaguely in the direction we'd come. "Needed an outing. My daily driver is a vintage Beetle convertible they asked me to display."

"Show but no go, right?" Gordon shared an inside joke with the Camaro's owner.

It was a good-natured rib I'd gotten used to during my ownership. "You're right there, you don't drive a bug to arrive first. But you do arrive in style." If I wanted to arrive first, I had the Goldstar. I could tell him that but I didn't want this opportunity to converse with him and Tiffany to descend into an ego fight.

"Style is okay," he acknowledged. "Tiffany, what do you think? Are you a speed or slow stylist?" He squeezed her waist.

"I like substance. Fast or slow, as long as I get there." She winked at me.

Gordon grimaced. "I heard you visited Jolene's ranch."

We walked slowly along the line of cars. "I did. She's got an impressive operation. Lots of work but I can see it's her passion."

"I wish I could help her out occasionally but I can't. She understands and deep down, I think she's grateful to make it on her own."

"You must be proud. Of Lawrence as well. I saw a picture of her and her brother, in their teens, I'd guess. On a tropical vacation. Oahu?"

Gordon knelt beside a Corvette and sighted down its side. "The early ones were never entirely smooth," he commented. "Oahu it was. We had a condo there for years."

"Another loss, like the car?" He'd either tell me or bristle.

"The car went to fund a second call for funds from Mendez. The condo became too hard to share with Elizabeth."

"She didn't like me being there, even after the separation," said Tiffany. She might look bored with the cars but she was paying attention.

"Tiffany's right."

"Elizabeth didn't want it for herself?"

"I'd taken a credit line on it for Mendez's third call. By the time his scheme sewered, the bank got the condo. Our joint share in Mendez's property had gone south. I'd gone into rehab for my back muscles and Elizabeth had gone to jail."

Time for the question I hadn't asked the first time. "Did the police ever ask you about Mendez's shooting?"

"Sure they did. I told them I might've had reason at one time but that was too long ago to hold such a vicious grudge."

"And Elizabeth?"

"She's one to hold anger longer than me but I can't imagine her pulling the trigger on Mendez. She'd like him pilloried but I doubt she'd even hold a gun again. I was drunk and in severe pain, lying on our garage floor after being shot. The one thing I remember above all else, was her crying and saying, 'I'm sorry, I'm sorry.'"

I glanced at Tiffany to see how she was taking this dredged up past. She held onto Gordon's arm, supporting him. She caught me looking at her. "She might have been sorry," said Mrs. Rudge the second, "but she still did it. There's capacity within her to do harm. She might not pick up a gun but there's poison in her mind."

Tiffany tugged Gordon away from us. She said, "Don't ask any more questions, Mr. Farina. Elizabeth is no longer our problem or concern."

"That was fun," said Jonas when they were beyond earshot.

I watched the couple walk further down the line of cars, arm in arm. "He has reason to hold in a lot of hate. But he seems more resigned than resentful." Today anyway. His previous rant about having to live on a boat came back to me. Which guy was he? Could the angry one pull a trigger on Mendez, picturing his ex-wife while he did?

THE REMAINDER OF THE day, evening and Sunday morning passed with two buddies enjoying a beach town different from their own.

"I can't believe there is a skateboard museum," said Jonas.

I read the sign. "Believe it. It's open. Maybe they have preserved bits of scab from our thrashing days."

They didn't but it was still cool. Skateboard art wasn't restricted to riding innovations but included board graphics, shapes and clothing. The history of the sport made a compelling narrative for me.

"If we were twenty years younger, we could make the pilgrimage to Dogtown and join a gang," I said.

Jonas bought a t-shirt. "I'll wear the dream instead."

Santa Cruz had provided much needed distraction and I got some info on the Rudges to add to the case. Jonas and I had a great dinner, alcohol-free for me. We headed home, top down and clinging to a youthful memory of doing the drive so many times in our teens.

Night fell as I parked the bug and retreated to my digs. Two messages.

The first, from Ynez, added to my elevated spirit. "Hi Clay, I'm back from the field trip, exhausted and buoyant. We harvested some great data. Just wanted to share. I'll call you Monday." Ynez sounded exactly as she described her condition.

The second, not so uplifting. It was work. "Clay, it's Colin Marsh. I received an interesting comment on this week's series. Thought you might like to read it. Here's the gist. 'The Herald is right to expose these schemers as scammers. They care little for how lives can be destroyed and dreams abandoned. It isn't lifestyle, it's family. It's lost vacations and abandoned friendships, thanks to people like Mendez.' Sound familiar? I think it's the same person who sent in the tip that started all this. Let's chat Monday at the Herald office."

I added my weekend notes to the cork board and sat with a scotch to one side, looking through the patio doors to the ocean, my glance flicking back to the board between each sip. I got up and took down the two texts comprising the tip-off and Marsh's latest. He was right, they likely were from the same source. I began to suspect who the source was. Another meeting for tomorrow.

Chapter 27

Monday morning broke with the phone shrieking.

"Hello?"

"It's Dennis. Did I wake you?"

"No, I had to answer the phone anyway." My mouth tasted like cat fur. I didn't own a cat. Nor was I owned by one.

"Very funny. You know the Carmel Valley Airport?"

"Yeah, sure. Where are you taking me?"

"Just get out here as fast as you can. Legally, of course."

"I've got some calls I want to make." I'd promised Elizabeth Rudge a follow-up and I wanted to ask Marsh about syndication profits.

"Forget them." Dennis was not in a delaying mood.

"Okay. I'll be there in half an hour. Where do I find you?"

"You'll see me."

I rinsed hair and teeth, tugged on sweats and my brand-new t-shirt.

Thirty-two minutes later, I understood what Dennis meant about finding him. There were half a dozen cop cars, an ambulance and two official non-patrol cars parked at various angles near the tower. I saw Mendez's Bentley as well, front doors wide open.

I parked. By the time I got close to the ambulance, it was pulling out, in no rush, no flashing lights or siren.

Dennis waved me through the warning tape. "It's Mendez," he said. I noted the evidence markers on the ground beside the Bentley. And the dark stains on the seat.

"Senior? How bad? When? What?" The ambulance's sedate pace implied the worst. Or the best? Another warning.

"You should be a reporter. Yeah, Senior. As bad as it gets. He's dead. Shot. Nine-millimeter this time. The heavier caliber was fatal. Looks like they got him as he was getting into his car from a flight."

"Where was he? Any idea?"

"Phoenix. We talked to his charter pilot. They'd made the flight a dozen times in the last six months. He was parking the plane and never heard the shots."

"What time?" I looked across the tarmac to a fleet of private planes. A person could hide behind the under carriage of any of them if they knew the victim was coming in.

"The plane touched down at three-fifty a.m. I give Mendez ten minutes before leaving the plane to walk to his car. The shooter was waiting. Got into the car with him, closed the door to muffle the sound and pumped him twice in the head. Shooter's probably got splashback on him or her. Or had. Burned or destroyed by now if it's as premeditated as it appears."

"Who called it in?"

"The pilot." Dennis pointed to a guy sitting in the back of a cruiser. "He came to check on him when he saw the car hadn't moved but the dome light was on and the passenger door open."

I visualized Dennis' re-creation. "The shooter got in. They knew more than Mendez's schedule; they knew him and Mendez knew the attacker."

Dennis nodded. "That's the way we figure it at the moment. Any ideas?"

"Consider the first attack a warning," I said. "It didn't take. I think Mendez is, was, pulling a fresh retread of his buying a troubled development with other people's money in Arizona. This time was too much for our attacker, if it was the same one. Will you notify the Mrs. and Junior?"

Dennis shook his head. "The Chief gets that lovely task."

"Will he talk to Diaz or Marsh at the Herald?"

"Marsh is on his way. I phoned him fifteen minutes after you. I wanted your take first."

I didn't tell him about Marsh's second letter which I'd connected to the initial accusation. My tip suspect might or might not be the shooter, I doubted they were but I couldn't figure a motive for the second letter. To up the rancor further against Mendez? Given his fate not long after Colin received the text, it hardly seemed necessary. Tipster was not the murderer. "I'd put protection around Elizabeth Rudge. Oscar Jr.'s going to be looking for a target."

"Good point."

Dennis left me with the Bentley. Mendez hadn't taken repercussions seriously enough.

I paced back and forth, trying to place any one of the people I'd talked with at this scene with a gun. Waiting for Mendez in the dark before dawn, getting into the car, closing the door, perhaps raving at him and when the verbal rage was spent, pulling the trigger. Twice against Oscar Mendez's head. Geezus.

Marsh came toward me. "You just passing by?" he asked.

"No. Dennis called me before he called you." Dennis was still on his cruiser radio so I filled Marsh in.

He made notes but his movements were stiff. Shock. At the deed or at his potential part in it. I doubted he'd done the deed but his articles may have pushed someone over reason's edge.

"Colin, this is an awkward time, but does the Herald syndicate your columns?"

"Sometimes. Felicia tries but more often than not we don't get circulated outside the bay area. Maybe Santa Cruz and Salinas."

"Any extra money in it?" How sensational did it have to be? How far would a paper go to generate larger interest?

"If there is, I don't see it. Goes into the pool."

"You try it on your own?"

"Yeah, once or twice."

He hadn't stopped making notes during our conversation.

"We're sending an officer to Elizabeth Rudge's home." Dennis nodded to Marsh. "What do you think?"

"I think I don't like the news business very much," said Marsh.

"Yeah," said Dennis. "There are days when I don't much like being a cop, either."

I didn't join in the regret circle. If I didn't like what I did most of the time, I wouldn't be doing it. My next task for the day, now completely revised, could be nasty too. But I had to start wrapping up as much as I could. Let the cops do the science for the crime scene, maybe they'd turn up evidence or a witness and save me stretching my brain to figure out who. If not, stretching my brain was good exercise.

I borrowed Marsh's phone, walked thirty or forty feet away with my back to him and called Pops. "Morning. I'm at Carmel Valley Airport. I need to tell you in person what's going on. Can you ask Roger Schopff to meet you and me? Preferably at his office, not yours."

"How urgent is this?" Pops asked.

"Very. I'll take a chance and see you in town in half an hour." I returned the phone. "Thanks."

I tugged Dennis aside from everyone's earshot. "I think I should let Elizabeth's lawyer know what happened. I'm going to try to meet with Roger and Pops as soon as I get back to town. Is that okay with you?"

"The lawyer should be alerted, Elizabeth will no doubt be in touch with him anyway. Tell him and your dad to keep it quiet for a day. Marsh'll be under the same time restriction. I'd like to see you later at the station. The forensic team will wrap up here. I'd like a list of possible suspects from you."

"Pick up a phone book."

"Wise ass."

"I'm serious. The line is long. Mendez touched a lot of lives, few in a good sense. Find out what he was doing in Phoenix and who he met with. I can give you one name to start. Colleen Axford. She's an independent investment manager. Her associate told me she was in Phoenix signing an exclusive marketing deal with a scheme that fit Mendez's pattern. I don't know for certain he was involved but see what you can shake out."

"Will do. Thanks, Clay."

I hoped I hadn't fingered a woman I had never met for a rough time with the cops.

POPS AND ROGER WERE waiting for me. My dad hadn't knotted his tie yet.

"What's so urgent, Clay?" Pops' tone hadn't mellowed from our encounter on Friday over the Whartons.

I couldn't ease into this. At least it wasn't my fault. I was the leg man, not the trigger man. "Mendez was shot and killed before dawn after he landed on a private charter from Phoenix."

Pops' displeasure evaporated. Roger paled.

I added, "We can't spread this until the police are finished their preliminaries but I thought Roger should know. Elizabeth may need protection from Oscar Jr., given the Herald's articles about her."

"You're right," said Roger. "She's an innocent figure in this."

Pops didn't say anything. I waited for a minute, then I said, "Not entirely."

Four eyes stared at me. "Explain," said Pops.

"Colin Marsh and the Herald have received numerous comments, rants and threats as a result of his columns on Mendez in particular and the lack of punishment for his type in general. A new one contained some specific comments I tagged and bore a similar syntax to the initial tip-note."

"The same person who alleged Elizabeth's involvement in Mendez's previous attack is still mad. You're not saying she actually was the attacker?" Roger summed it up neatly.

"No, I'm pretty certain she wasn't. I do suspect she wrote the first letter."

"What?" Pops exploded.

"Clay, you and I both heard Dr. Tam," said Roger. "Elizabeth's temper is under control. Gordon is out of her life and away from her anger."

"But her lifestyle is not what it was. She knows she paid the price in jailtime for shooting Gordon. She didn't expect the financial fallout to be so significant. More critically, in my opinion, she didn't expect the societal descent to be so severe. She's lost standing, popularity, an opulent residence for entertaining her former friends as shallow as she was. She gave up the Hawaiian retreat. She gave up undivided affection from her children. Hell, the son moved to Denver to get away from the stress of trying to love both parents embroiled in a bitter and public fight."

"Why would she write the letter?" Pops repeated.

"Because she turned her anger from Gordon to the man who ruined Gordon's economic status, and thus hers. Mendez. She wanted him to suffer and settle the lawsuits. Marsh's renewed publicity was the start. Elizabeth banked on Mendez's case being moved along in the hope she could recoup some of what she lost."

"It seems far-fetched," said Roger. "I'd feel foolish trying to sell such a scheme to a judge or jury and frankly, I'm not sure she has the capacity to plan it."

"Her loss of status eats at her every day. She has the time to stew and finally she hit on a way to bring Mendez to justice. I don't know if she thought he'd be physically attacked again. It's a question for her. The police will figure it out soon enough, once they go through Marsh's files. We should know her answer first."

Pops let out a long, whistling breath. "Who draws the short straw?"

"It should be me," said Roger. "With Clay."

Pops looked to me.

"I agree, Pops. It won't help nail the killer but it does accomplish what you asked me to do. Clear her in the first attack."

Roger picked up the phone. "It's Roger, would you connect me with Elizabeth Rudge, please?" He hung on for a minute then spoke again. "Elizabeth, it's Roger Schopff. You heard? How are you doing? Are they there now?" He held a hand over the mouthpiece. "A policewoman is parked across the street." He spoke to Elizabeth again. "Is the car unmarked? Officer in uniform or not? I think you and I should meet. I'll bring Clay Farina with me. We'll speak to the officer when we get there. Twenty minutes or less."

"She sounds shaken," said Roger. "The policewoman got there half an hour ago, introduced herself, and told Elizabeth that Mendez was dead. No details."

Pops laid a hand on my arm. "Clay, go easy with her. We know she didn't kill Mendez and she's still our client."

I wanted to protest. Her innocence wasn't proven beyond all doubt but he was right. She was our client and trusted us. I'd be challenging that trust with one serious accusation as it was. I hoped her reaction would be more reasonable than Dr. Wharton's, the last time I confronted someone with the truth.

We parked behind the ghost car. Roger got out first and stood by the window, talking to the officer. He nodded and I got out and joined them. Elizabeth would receive my promised second visit after all.

"How much can I tell Mrs. Rudge?" I asked.

The cop said, "Mendez is dead, that's it for now. No mention of how or that it was homicide."

"How do you explain your presence?"

"Precautionary, nothing more until I'm told otherwise." The cop shrugged. "I don't like the lie any more than you. It insults her intelligence and mine but until I get more direction, that's the line. And don't ask her for an alibi."

"I'm her lawyer and an officer of the court," said Roger. "Don't insult my intelligence."

"I'm not trying to. A reminder for your partner here." She looked at me.

"She's right, Roger. I could cross a legal line without thinking or knowing. Not that many single people could have a solid alibi for four a.m. Hell, I don't. We'll keep our discussion away from the murder details."

Roger and I walked up the driveway. The front door opened and Elizabeth beckoned us in.

"Thank you for coming Roger, I wasn't sure I should call you or not. The officer was vague and worrisome at the same time. I don't understand why I need protection."

We sat in the sunroom where I'd spoken with her last week.

Roger said, "Oscar Mendez is dead. The police can't be certain there isn't actually some link between you and Mendez, this putting you in possible danger as well. The cop outside is precautionary."

"They think I had something to do with his death?"

"Not directly involved with his death but tenuously connected."

Her hands clenched into little fists. "How did he die? What's the reason?"

"The police aren't releasing any details yet," said Roger.

I took my cue. "The link for the moment is the tip-off note and the articles in the Herald."

"The paper is as responsible as me, then. They don't do enough when people lose their savings and go too far after the fact."

"I won't argue the point," I said. "I agree with you. They didn't do enough when Mendez was initially accused of financial dirty deeds." I looked at Roger. He nodded. I glanced at the carpet for a moment then met Elizabeth's gaze. "That's why you wrote the two letters. Not to bring you into the light, but to shine it back on him. You wanted justice. And more."

She unclenched her hands. "I wanted justice. I wanted him to suffer the way I had. The way my children have. The way so many others have. And he lives in luxury on our dollars."

She'd accomplished justice, though perhaps not the way she'd planned. Mendez had destroyed lives but I looked around and Elizabeth Rudge wasn't living on crackers and ketchup packet soup. I wasn't certain I entirely forgave her motive.

"Do the police know about the notes? Is that why they're outside? Not to protect me but to watch me?"

Roger shook his head. "No, the protection is real enough. Protect you from the press or curiosity seekers. The police may work slowly but if Clay made the link, they'll get to it eventually. You could help them by telling them you wrote the tip. I'll be there with you and arrange beforehand minimum, if any, repercussions."

She looked at me. "How did you figure it out? Even Jolene didn't suspect."

I pointed to the abbreviated family photo on her mantle. "The Oahu property, the second letter and connecting the pieces you just confirmed. You use the phrase 'thanks to...'. I wasn't entirely certain until you acknowledged it."

"What now?" she asked.

"Wait for my call," said Roger. "Have you talked to your family?"

"I left Jolene a message."

"Do you have a friend to wait with you?" I asked.

"Yeah. I'll ask Mary next door. She's the closest thing I have to a friend since the divorce." Bitterness crept into her voice for a moment, then she perked up. "I talked to Lawrence as well, he's flying from Denver tomorrow."

I said, "I have to ask, why did you bring Pops and me into it?"

"Your dad has mentioned you a couple of times. He said if I ever needed 'special' help, come to him and see if your skills fit the need. I thought you might just find out who shot Mendez and the trial would garner the publicity I sought." Elizabeth trembled.

Roger made the move and put an arm around her shoulders. Not my special skill, not this time. She had a part in Mendez's death. Small, maybe whoever killed him would've done it anyway but I kept coming back to the concept of catalyst. I felt anger towards her because my own actions had precipitated Buddy's death. Again, his life trajectory was unavoidable. Old age wasn't in his deck.

Roger and I stayed with her until she gathered the strength to call her neighbor.

Back in my car, we sat and watched the neighbor enter Elizabeth's front door. "Do you think the D.A. will press charges against her?" I asked.

Roger tapped his hands on the vertical dash. "Not if I can persuade them to keep it simple. I'll make the case that bringing Elizabeth into a murder trial would unnecessarily confuse a judge and jury. A good defense lawyer could render a straightforward conviction into a jumbled dismissal, a mistrial at the very least."

"If the police find the killer."

"There is that." He turned to me. "You still may be her best hope. Work on it. Something you turn up might be the clue needed."

"Clues and evidence aren't always the same. But I'm glad you feel this way. I'm not sure Pops wants me to carry on further." I pulled in front of Roger's office.

He got out and rested his hands on the door sill. "Convince him."

Or proceed until reprimanded. The strategy in Dr. Wharton's case brought the desired result but the collateral damage was on my head. Had I learned enough not to create more unwanted blowback this time? Life's journey was about learning from your mistakes. I gained wisdom daily.

Chapter 28

Pops closed his office door and we sat staring at each other for a minute.

I broke the ice and related Elizabeth's mood and Roger's evaluation of any charges going forward.

"I'm baffled by her intensity," said Pops. "I thought she'd paid her penalty for shooting Gordon, settled into her new life, recognizing she was better off without him and all the flash than with him and being cuckolded on a regular basis."

"She'd lived with it so long before the shooting and divorce, it was a negative reinforcement she depended upon. There's my four bucks' worth of psychology."

"You're probably right, Clay. I'll double your estimate."

I pulled out the list Milt had made.

"I visited Axford's office. She was out. In Phoenix, according to her colleague, tying up an exclusive arrangement to market this." I showed him the details based on the preliminary prospectus I'd seen from said colleague. "It rings so Mendez, doesn't it?"

Pops studied the artwork. He picked up his phone and started making calls. Twenty minutes later, he disconnected. "It's Mendez, all right. Or was."

"Do you think he backed out on her monopoly?"

"You might want to suggest it to the police. I know she runs a few high-risk deals but she doesn't misrepresent."

"Not a crook, in other words."

"I wouldn't say so, no."

Milt's take was in contrast. I changed gears. "Mendez, from everything I can gather, wasn't a womanizer so that likely eliminates love or hate for motives. Leaving money."

"The trail to follow, if you can find it."

"Like all the suspects, many trails lead to Mendez. Unraveling the correct one leading away from him isn't beaconing to me. But I want to keep on the case, for Elizabeth's sake. Are you okay with that?"

"Yes. Work with the police, not around them."

I couldn't fully commit. "We'll see. I don't want to be giving Dennis a list of twenty suspects and pissing them all off. I need some time on my own to nudge the key from behind the curtain."

"Okay. Keep me posted daily. More often if in specific doubt." Pops checked his watch. "I've got a tee-off for three o'clock. Use this office if you require."

I remembered Armand Moore's story about his alleged eavesdropped conversation at Sea Grass. "How many other wealth management firms are members?"

"None," said Pops. "We have an unwritten agreement to limit ourselves to one club each and not to overlap."

Another conclusion I'd have to change. "That must be difficult, given the number of competitors in the region."

"There is no shortage of clubs, either. Some smaller firms aren't forced to adhere through mutual agreement but the larger ones like us honor the accord. Why the interest in golf suddenly?"

"One of Mendez's victims claims he overheard a tip from someone at your club a year or two back. He thought at least one of the guys pumping Mendez's name was an investment consultant."

"That doesn't narrow the field. It could have been a guest or an independent broker. Anyone with the drive to pass the required exams can offer investment services. You'd be surprised at the number of clients we get, after their neighbor, accountant or barber's brother-in-law has disappointed or gone into another business."

"But it could have been someone with Farina-Black." Or Moore could be lying.

"Not with regard to Mendez. We put him on a no-go list long ago."

"Any former Farina-Black employees? Any departures in the last year?"

"Not on the advisor side, no. Stability is one of our mainstays. We want our clients to deal with the same individuals through their tenure. Our demographics run from my age to young bucks in their twenties. The senior staff mentor and co-advise. Anything else?"

"No. Thanks."

Pops left. I called Dennis Levi.

"Did you get anything from Colleen Axford?"

"She's still in Phoenix, due back this evening. I have an appointment with her tomorrow."

"What about other flights yesterday from Phoenix. Commercial or charters?"

"Haven't checked. Why?"

"Just speculating. She could've flown back ahead of Mendez, done the deed, chartered or taken an early morning flight to Phoenix and been there when you called."

"A stretch but worth getting the manifests. It would have to be commercial. Mendez's flight was the only private one from Arizona all weekend."

"I'd like to look over the names when you get them."

"I'll let you know."

"How did the news go down with Mrs. Mendez? And Junior?"

"She's devastated. Junior was racing at Riverside. She called him while the chief was there. He's already on the road home. We'll warn him to not make any assumptions about guilt. If he's got an idea, he'll give the lead to us."

"Can you trust him?"

"No. We'll watch him. And make certain he knows he's under surveillance."

"Any chance he could've made a high-speed run from Riverside and back?"

"Always a possibility. Riverside police are digging on their end. Why would you think patricide?"

"I'm grasping. Junior's cash burn rate is eating in to what his father had left. He can slow down, which is unlikely, wait for the courts to seize and re-distribute what his dad had left, or try to mortgage his future against the inheritance."

"Grasping is right. But I'd already proposed a similar scenario to the team. I've got to run, if you've nothing else."

"Go. Call me on the flight lists."

Now what? I tried Ynez. Answering machine. "I'll be at the Bay Grill for the rest of this afternoon consulting with my conscience. His name is Jonas. Call me there or join us after school, if you can. I want to hear more about your weekend. Mine had highs and lows."

JONAS LISTENED ATTENTIVELY to my retelling the Mendez update. "It'll be on the news by tomorrow but keep it tight until then."

"Who am I going to tell?"

"Just doing my duty for Dennis. You never know when a listener might get the idea there's advantage to be gained from knowing before it's general news. I'm breaking a trust with Dennis by informing you, but if it helps my reasoning, I'll justify it. Do you have any insights I've missed?"

We settled in, Jonas with his wine, soda and lime for me. I went through my list of knowns and unknowns, slanting the motive on the money side but not ignoring passion if there was something I'd missed.

An hour later, we were no closer but at least my instincts were confirmed by a mind I respected.

Then the day brightened considerably.

"Hi."

Ynez sat beside me as I gathered my cards and slipped them in my pocket. I made the introductions. She sniffed my drink. "That doesn't smell alcoholic."

"I can change that. Will you join us for dinner?"

"And wine. The field trip was great but we have to run them dry. I took a cab here."

"We can take out and imbibe at my place," I offered.

Jonas looked embarrassed at my awkward suggestion. Hell, I was embarrassed after I said it.

Ynez took my comment in stride. "No, we'll eat drink and be merry here, I think."

Pressure off. I was almost relieved. Then I looked at her profile in the bar's light. No, I wasn't relieved. I wanted to know this woman.

"What were you boys doing with those cards? From your board?"

"Discussing relationships, betrayals, and new connections," said Jonas.

Betrayals. How'd he land on that? I let it corkscrew into my hind-mind for vetting. Unsure if it could survive wine and unrequited lust, I scribbled the word on a fresh card and inserted it with the others.

"Now," I said. "You will tell us how our state ecology can be saved from well-meaning but lazy clods like us."

Ynez's excitement poured forth. She linked the complexities together between emissions, power grids, ocean currents, temperature changes, ice-packs.

I thought my problems with the case were overwhelming. "How do you not throw your hands in the air and cry, 'enough already'?"

She paused, inhaling deeply. Regaining her breath, she said, "Too many people have. The challenge is to break it down into pieces which an individual can control. Protests, marches, shaming and the like saturate us. The message gets tuned out. I encourage my students to lead by example. We studied desert plants which thrive in the heat. How can we harvest them? And for what? We're going to be busy."

Jonas swirled his glass. "The root problem always returns to too many people to sustain over the long term, does it not?"

Ynez nodded. "Unfortunately, that's an issue no one dares to speak aloud. When's the last time you heard a politician or a tree-hugger preach population control?"

"Or advertisers," I added. "Reduce the number of people and you reduce the number of consumers."

"Subsistence farming for two percent," said Jonas. "Starvation for the rest. It's not a popular nor perhaps a possible solution."

"A good plague?" I suggested.

"We're too good at fighting them," said Ynez. "This isn't going to be resolved by us tonight. How's your case?"

"Getting complicated," I said. "More news tomorrow or Wednesday. Let's eat while we can without feeling crushing guilt."

Chapter 29

Dennis was still waiting on the flight manifests when I called him Tuesday morning.

"I talked to Colleen Axford," he said. "I'm on my way to her office now. Would you care to join me?"

"I would. If I can ask a question or two."

"Keep it focused on the case. Meet me there."

He was sitting outside her office when I pulled in behind his cruiser. We entered together. Axford was older than I expected. Why I expected different I couldn't say. She was a small woman in her early fifties, streaky blond hair pulled in a tight ponytail, heavy on the makeup but probably attractive under the paint. Her smile was a thousand bucks. We weren't interrogators, we were potential clients.

Dennis introduced us both. She held my hand for a fraction longer than mere courtesy. "Farina. Any relation to Glen?"

"My father. But I'm not your competition. I'm in private investigations."

"You can spy on me all you like, Clay. There's room enough for all of us. Sheriff Levi, how can I help you?"

"Tell me about Oscar Mendez and your trip to Phoenix."

She shifted her glance between the two of us. Trying to figure out Dennis' role or mine? "Should I begin with why you're asking?"

Dennis sighed. He was going to tell her. It seemed only fair not to risk an entrapment charge. I watched her. Eyes, lips, body language.

"Mr. Mendez was killed early yesterday morning."

Her shock looked genuine to me but she was a professional salesperson. The good ones were always in control. "Killed? How? Why?"

"The how is still confidential. I was hoping you might shed some light on the why. When did you last speak with him?"

It took Colleen a moment to compose. Again, I thought it genuine.

"I spoke with him Sunday, mid-afternoon." She wasn't giving away anything extra.

"What was that conversation about?"

"We signed an agreement. I don't know where his death leaves that. I'm granted exclusive right to market his latest development outside Phoenix."

One to me, confirmed.

"Was your relationship amicable?"

"Obviously." She let the smoothness slip for a moment. "Yes, I would say our relationship was very amicable."

"When did you know he was giving you exclusivity?" I asked.

"We discussed it last month, here in my office. He showed me his plans and some draft brochure content. I wanted to look the prospect over in person. I did so on Saturday and we reached verbal terms then. Sunday, we closed the deal. I wanted another day to take pictures and talk to the contractors. Which I did all yesterday."

"Was anyone else in the running?" I asked.

"I assume so but Oscar's style wasn't to specify the competition."

"Did that guarantee him the best deal?" Dennis asked.

"It guaranteed him the best partner," she said.

"You knew Mendez's reputation," I said. "Did that bother you? Were you leery of being associated with him?" I looked at the impressive but small office.

"That is why I went to see the development. This one was solid. I'm convinced of that. I was willing to take the risk."

"Were your clients?" Dennis asked, before I could.

"I am always honest with my investors, Sheriff. Ask Clay, here. His father's firm doesn't mislead. Neither do I."

I'd let that lie. It was true about Pops but I had no idea of her track record. Other than Milt's intimation that she balanced on honesty's cusp.

We heard the jingle from the front door. Colleen looked through the glass door of her office. "Gavin. My associate."

"I met him last week," I said. "Full associate?"

"I'm mentoring. He's young but ambitious. He has the knowledge but I can't tell if he has the sales gift yet."

She looked at me for confirmation one way or the other. My opinion wasn't worth squat about Gavin so I didn't judge. But if she were as competent as she appeared, she'd know if he could make the grade before she hired him.

"Thank you for your time, Ms. Axford. If I need anything else, I'll call." Dennis stood and I followed.

"I'll be available."

"I may have another question or two at some point as well," I said.

She veneered the million-dollar smile on as she shook my hand. "Of course. Gavin can answer if I'm not here."

Already demoted to the probationary associate. If I needed what I wanted from her, I'd need bait.

Outside, we stood by my car. "Get anything out of that?" I asked.

"I was going to ask you the same. Ms. Axford stands to lose a lot with Mendez's death. Can't see a motive for her to do the deed."

"Not unless there's some wrinkle in that contract she has and I doubt Mendez would commit to anything which benefited a partner upon his death."

Dennis' phone buzzed. He scrolled through the message. "We have the flight manifests you wanted."

"I'll follow you to the station."

I TROLLED THE LISTS of incoming Phoenix flights from Saturday and Sunday. Sunday's 1730 hours on a small regional had one name I recognized. Someone who had every reason to be in Phoenix over the weekend. Maybe more than one or two reasons. There were private airports other than the one Mendez used so Axford still could have flown into Santa Cruz or Salinas, done the deed, then flown back to take her commercial flight today.

"Thanks, Dennis."

"Do you mind telling me what, if anything, you see?"

"Not yet. I need to do some checking, then I'll bring you in. I don't want to shake the tree until I'm sure the monkey's home. Besides, you've got all the forensic science to wade through. You'll probably find the killer before I do."

"Flattering but don't count on it."

My first stop was municipal hall, Land Titles department. I could have used a private lien search firm but I didn't know how long that would take so I buttoned my mind into government bureaucracy mode and dove in.

It went smoother than I expected. Three hours and two line-ups later, I had my information.

My second task was phoning Pops' confidential secretary. The information took her five minutes. "Audrey," I said, "you should work for the city. You'd render fourteen people redundant and save us all mega-tax dollars."

The info led me to a small marina. I had the slip number, B-15, but no description. I checked the For Sale listings on the dock board. B-15 was there, open to offers. No surprise, just disappointment that I was getting closer.

I pressed the buzzer and a marina hand appeared on the other side of the fence. "Can I help you?"

"I wanted to take a look at B-15. For sale, you know it?"

He pulled a remote from his pocket and pointed it at the gate, not me. I tried to look prosperous as I walked toward him with the rolling gait of an experienced yachtsman. He didn't seem to notice.

"Third one on your right, down there."

I obeyed his directions and pretended to give the boat a practised appraisal. I spent twenty minutes on the charade and then tracked him down.

"What's the scoop? She seaworthy? Maintenance up to date?"

"It'll need a mechanical check. Are you serious?"

"For the right price, I could be."

"The price will get more right every day. The owner's behind on his moorage fees and who knows what else. Are you a fisherman or just want to cruise?"

"I have a friend in Santa Cruz. Thought it might be more fun to visit her with a boat and go out on the bay for the odd overnight gig. I hate the weekend highway snarl. How long for that boat to make the trip?"

"It's a plugger, take you over an hour. The overnight thing works though, saw it come in early yesterday, around seven."

Bingo? Yahtzee? "Are you sure of the time?"

"Quarter of an hour after I began my shift." He wiped his hands on a rag stuffed in his belt. "If you want something quicker than driving, check out the launch in F-11. Not as much cabin room but you could overnight and get where you want to go much faster."

"Thanks, I'll have a look." I wandered over to F-11 and did the same appraisal but my mind wasn't in it. I was picturing the sequence. I had land routes to time and then I'd be sure.

I clocked the drive from the marina to the private airport where Mendez had been killed. Time of death was known from the pilot's touchdown. I walked from the most likely parking spot, one where the vehicle wouldn't be picked up on surveillance, nor the driver. Added them together and figured how far out into the bay one could get and be back by 7:15 a.m. It'd work.

All I needed now was proof. Any kind of proof.

Chapter 30

On Wednesday morning, I laid it out for Dennis. He agreed with the conjectures and the fact I had no proof. Neither had the police.

He wasn't all negative. "It gives us a start. If I can get a search warrant, we may dig up supporting evidence."

"Physical search of house, boat and car," I said. "A records search on property finances and banking as well. I hope I'm not wasting your time. Hard evidence might be absent and I could still be convinced I'm right." I reclined in his guest chair and stared at the station house ceiling. My peripheral board floated past. Snap. I pulled my name cards and found the one. "I might have an eye and ear witness for one of the links."

Dennis read the name. "Armand Moore. Who the hell is he?"

"A Mendez victim who's taking the hard route back to prosperity; he's working for it. I need to get him in the same room." I looked around the grim décor inside the Sheriff's portion of the courthouse. "Not here. Pops' place. We round up the herd."

I wrote out the list of attendees I wanted present. "Can you lean officially to get them all there?"

"I'll have to clear it with the chief but yeah. When? I'll need a day to get the warrants carried out. When the suspect isn't home."

"I'll take care of contacting Moore and the Rudges. If they're a go for Thursday, we'll shoot for two o'clock."

"Don't use that word."

I gave him my puzzled look.

"*Shoot.*"

"Sorry, slip of the tongue."

When I got home, I pinned the cards back to the corkboard and went through it one more time. Staring wouldn't prevent me from reviewing it sixteen times that night but writing it down might. I scribbled it all out in sequence.

My first phone call was a failed success to the Securities Commission. Percy Oaks, self-important Commission bully, had left our area. He was on special assignment in San Diego. Upon my further questioning, I was advised he'd been so since Monday afternoon. He'd split as soon as the news about Mendez began to circulate. What a toad.

Relieved Oaks no longer threatened me or my investigation, I made my second call. "Mr. Moore, this is Clay Farina, we've met twice in your driveway. I need a big favor from you. Can you meet me at my father's office Thursday at 1:30?" I'd need time to prepare him for what I had in mind.

"My wife needs the car to shuttle the kids."

They were down to one vehicle. "No problem. I'll pick you up around one o'clock."

"I'll be ready."

"Great. I can't promise anything beyond possible closure on Mendez." I hoped he wouldn't change his mind after tomorrow's news on Mendez's killing came to light.

I gave him the address and said I'd call Thursday morning to confirm.

My next call took five rings before being answered. "Jolene? It's Clay Farina. You heard? She told you about the letters? That's why I'm calling. Roger will take care of your mother's lapse in judgment but I can maybe give you more than that. For her, you, your dad and your brother. I'd like you and Gordon to be at my father's office Thursday. No, Tiffany doesn't need to be there and I'd think there'd be less chance of fireworks if she wasn't. You agree? Good. Can you keep the tension reasonable between your parents in the same room? Again, good. I thought you might if anyone could. Thanks, Jolene."

My penultimate call was to Roger Schopff. "Roger, it's Clay. I'm arranging a bit of a case séance for Thursday. Can you bring Elizabeth and Lawrence to Pops' office at two? Let me know. Once she's committed, give her a head's up that Gordon will be there, with Jolene. If you could co-referee, that'd be excellent. Tell her it's the last time she'll need to be involved with the Mendez matter."

Final call. "Hi Pops. I think we're close. Dennis Levi and I would like to use your boardroom Thursday afternoon to tie the Mendez thing up. For the Rudges and the community at large. Two o'clock. Thanks. I'd like a non-official scribe to note everything. Can you ask Milt? Great. See you then. No, I haven't talked to Ynez since yesterday. Saturday? We'll be there if she's willing and available. I'll enjoy the chance to build some cobwebs."

DENNIS GOT HIS WARRANTS on Wednesday too late for the house and car search but carried out the boat exam without the owner's knowledge.

"Our timing was good," Dennis informed me. "Not so much on the evidence side. The owner'd asked for a full clean but the dockhand checked with his manager first, given the payment arrears situation. Manager told him to forget it unless the outstanding account was zeroed."

"No blood?" I asked.

"None. Here's an interesting fact. There's no anchor."

"That is interesting. Any sign of panic removal?"

"Rope wasn't cut, if that's what you mean. No anchor, no rope."

"There is evidence sitting at the bottom of the bay. Based on time available and boat speed, I'd say it's three or four thousand feet below the surface in the Monterey Canyon. No Abalone poacher is going to stumble across it. Maybe you'll do better with the car and house."

"We'll comb the house tomorrow when no-one's there. I think we'll save the car until after your assembly. No warning."

"Traffic camera searches for the time of Mendez's killing?"

"Generic cars. No readable licence plates. Our community is not well lit in the wee hours."

"How'd you make out with my attendee list? Everyone on board?"

"Yep. Curiosity is a great incentive. I didn't have to push at all."

"I'll see you tomorrow. Call me if you turn up anything at the house. Thanks, Dennis."

I called Ynez from home and made a date to meet at seven for dinner. This time at the Sea Grass club. I might as well try the gentrified impression route. And the menu fare was a notch up on the Bay Grill.

I WORE A SPORTSCOAT, no tie, navy slacks and black shoes. Ynez wore a mid-calf dress and yellow shoulder wrap. We were not in jeans and sweats, a comfortable change. Once in a while it refreshes the psyche to dress up. Second time in just over a week. I would become my father if I wasn't careful.

"Do you come here often?" she asked when we'd placed our drink orders.

"I was here for lunch the week before last and that was the first time in months. I have corporate guest privileges through Farina-Black."

Ynez turned to the windows. The outside green turf was illuminated here and there by carriage lamps. "Do you golf?"

"A condition to maintain my guest privilege is that I do not, under any circumstance, set foot or club on the course. I am what they call a 'human hazard'."

She giggled. "That bad?"

"That dangerous. Now you know. Is there anything you are abominable at?"

"Let's see. I tried skiing once. The trees are safer that I quit immediately. I couldn't understand it, I'm an above average bowler and I thought the skills would translate."

It was my turn to giggle. I was driving so I stopped at one beer with the meal. The giggles kept on despite my sobriety. It was a relaxing, charming evening. I needed the mental recess before tomorrow's confrontation. There was a chance I was wrong, thereby eroding Pops' faith in his agent and son, making myself look foolish, something I'd gotten used to over the years, and risking a person's reputation with false charges. I knew how that felt from the other side.

We drove home in the comfortable silence which blossoms suddenly when two strangers crack the shell.

"Call me tomorrow?" Ynez asked at her door.

"I will. Late afternoon. I've a case to finish or destroy after lunch."

"You didn't mention it this evening."

"Not worth mentioning this evening. We had too many other trivial issues to discuss."

She gave me a long kiss and hug before a 'goodnight'.

Chapter 31

I spent two hours Thursday morning reviewing, rehearsing and ensuring I hadn't missed anything material, or more importantly, anything contradictory to my case. It was how the lawyers on television did it, getting the performance down smooth so the logical elements could be presented compellingly.

I made my attendance confirmation calls. No last-minute bails to wreck my plan.

I had a fruit and protein smoothie for lunch, then drove to Armand Moore's place. He'd matched my dress code with his own blazer and tropical slacks.

I stared at his checkered deck shoes. "You keep a boat?"

"Fifteen-foot dinghy. Big enough for family outings, small enough to handle solo when I need a break. Upkeep's minimal and it reminds me I live by the ocean and should be grateful every day."

"I can't argue with that."

He stared at my pocket square.

I took out my 'tie-by-Samuel' to show him the full cloth. "It's supposed to be a tie but we're not in court today so I've affected it as decoration thus." I folded it and tucked it back in my breast pocket.

Armand chatted about his life growing up in the area on our drive in. He'd taught English briefly at a small college before deciding building houses and flipping them was more lucrative. He drifted into day-trading during the early 1990's real estate recession and not gone back to manual labor.

We slipped into Farina-Black's boardroom at one-thirty-five. I introduced him to Pops and Dennis then went through my attendee list for Armand. "I know it's a lot of names but you don't need to memorize them, just listen and watch. I'll introduce you as people arrive." I was ninety-five percent convinced Moore wasn't Mendez's final shooter. The fact he had a boat reduced it from yesterday's ninety-nine percent.

Dennis took a chair away from the boardroom table and sat with his notebook. Pops and Armand chatted about the latter's investment counsel, current and historical.

"I was my own advisor until I sunk everything into Mendez Inc. I'm using Greentree now," said Armand. "Not that I have a genuine portfolio but they've managed my debt well."

"I know Archie Kirk over there. They're a good shop." Pops knew everyone, it seemed.

Roger, Elizabeth and Lawrence were the first to arrive, escorted by Milt Canyon. Lawrence Rudge shared Jolene's build and rugged jaw. He was quiet in manner and voice. I eased Armand into the group as a fellow Mendez victim so they had chit-chat in common.

Colin Marsh entered with Colleen Axford. I slid Armand over to them, then turned as Gordon entered with Jolene. Gordon's voice carried across the room. "Larry, my boy. Good to see you." He made it clear that it was not 'good' to see his ex-wife with son but Jolene had apparently warned him to behave.

Jolene made eye contact with me then quickly shifted her gaze to my pocket adornment. "Looks like a Samuel," she said.

Good, my inside man at the ranch hadn't informed her about my visit and questions about her gun proficiency.

"I liked Samuel the first time I met him. When I visited Mendez, I hopped over the hills and dropped in. I couldn't leave without a tie." Jolene didn't question my story. She left to hug her brother and mother before returning to Gordon's side.

Oscar Mendez Jr. was the last to show. His bravado was gone. The loss of his father had hit him hard. Whether it was emotional or financial, I couldn't tell.

I let the crowd murmur for another ten minutes, getting water glasses from Pops and Milt and seeing that Armand circulated sufficiently.

"If we could take seats, ladies and gentlemen," I said. I remained standing at the end of the table, back to the window. "I thank everyone for coming today. This is not a joyous occasion. Like him or not, all present had an association with the late Oscar Mendez. I especially want to thank Oscar, his son, for attending. This is not an easy time for the family and I hope all present share in expressing our grief."

There were nods and more murmurs. Junior graciously acknowledged the gesture.

"To ensure we all know who is here, I'll ask each person around the table to introduce themselves and give a one-liner about who they are. Mr. Moore, could you begin?"

"Armand Moore, private investor."

"Roger Schopff, I'm Elizabeth's lawyer."

"Elizabeth Rudge, private investor with Farina-Black."

"Lawrence Rudge, son."

"Colin Marsh, columnist for the County Herald."

"Colleen Axford, wealth manager and investment counsel."

"Glen Farina, father to your host."

"Oscar Mendez Jr." He didn't need to add a liner.

"Milt Canyon, wealth manager here at Farina-Black and scribe for today."

I pointed to the corner beside me.

"Dennis Levi. County Sheriff."

I'd watched Moore's face as each person spoke. I circled the table, making regular eye contact with Moore. He nodded once. Whew. He'd either picked at random or his story was valid. I chose to believe the latter. Voice recognition might not stand up in a court of law but it pushed me forward.

"Oscar, some of the words today about your father may be uncomfortable. You can excuse yourself at any time."

"I know what my father was, Mr. Farina. This isn't easy but as the only son, I am the head of the family now and accept the responsibility which comes with that."

The wastrel becomes a man? "Your choice is a difficult but a strong one. I appreciate it. I won't encourage any one here to hold back due to your presence. Apologies to the Rudge family also for opening old wounds but it will lead to a conclusion."

I shifted my weight from foot to foot. "I was brought into this two and half weeks ago when Colin and Dennis each received an anonymous tip that the similarities between two shootings should be investigated. The tipster pointed out the same gun type had been used in two, seemingly unrelated incidents. One, the eight-month-old shooting, non-fatal, of Oscar Mendez Sr. outside his home in Carmel Valley. The second, five years ago when Elizabeth Rudge shot her then-husband, Gordon, in their garage. Again, I apologize but this letter and subsequent story in the Herald began a sequence of events. Colin, I'll ask you to pick up the narrative here and explain your reaction and subsequent actions."

Marsh cleared his throat. "I discussed the letter with my editor and Sheriff Levi. The Herald decided to publish the story but with a larger purpose in mind. We recounted the facts in the Rudge shooting and used it to examine the all-too-frequent marital abuse which still goes on in our society, years after the nasty publicity suffered by the Rudge family." He avoided eye contact with Gordon. "My second week of columns began with the kernel of the late Mr. Mendez's investment systems and their non-uniqueness. I then dug further into the fallout from his and similar schemes. How the securities regulators moved slowly, when they moved at all. Repercussions from actions, mostly self-inflicted and reactions."

"Leading to my father's death?" asked Oscar Jr.

"We'll come to that," I said. "Sheriff, can you describe the police response?"

Dennis rose and leaned on the window ledge beside me.

"We too were frustrated at the lack of progress we'd made in investigating the first attack on Mendez. A lot of people accused us of not trying hard due to the nature of his business and that he wasn't seriously injured. I assured him and his family we were always ready to follow up any clue they might turn up, any threat, any suspicious activity around them or their property. When we received the letter two weeks ago, we were more interested in the motive for the letter rather than giving credence to the allegation. Someone wanted us to put .22 and .22 together, so to speak."

I liked the word play but apparently no one else did, or they didn't get it. Philistines.

Dennis continued, "I contacted Elizabeth Rudge and advised her to talk to a lawyer or someone who could advise her. We kept the Mendez shooting file open but really the letter gave us little progress." He returned to his corner chair.

I spoke. "The letter had a more subtle purpose than casting suspicion on Elizabeth Rudge. Many investors, and some in this room, lost substantial portions of their assets, pride and lifestyle, due to their ill-advised holdings in certain opportunities offered through Mr. Mendez Sr. and his various holding companies. The letter writer was conceivably one of those, frustrated not at the lack of progress in finding Mendez's attacker but in the legal process of recouping some of their lost funds. They hoped renewed publicity would push the relevant government agencies and lawyers to get on with it.

"As you heard, Colin and his editor agreed and he penned a series of articles, first on Elizabeth's case, then on Mendez's operation. He expanded both situations to include the greater commonality. Many spouses endured what Elizabeth had with no aid to turn to and many investment schemes thrived while government watchdogs watched their own asses."

The room was uncomfortable. I felt bad for Elizabeth but she had started the engine. Gordon had sewn his own shroud while sewing oats about the county. "My father will pick up the story."

Pops leaned forward so all could see him. "Elizabeth called me after speaking with her daughter when Dennis advised her about the letter. She needed advice and I was grateful she thought of me as a friend first in the process. I asked her to meet in my office and called Roger Schopff, our associated counsel, to provide his support. We arrived at a three-part strategy which involved the efforts of my son, Clay. To absolutely clear her name and reputation, we proposed first identifying the letter-writer, second, proving Elizabeth could not have shot Mendez and best of all possible outcomes, find out who did." He reclined.

"Roger," I asked, "anything to add?"

He shook his head. "Not at this point."

"Gordon, can you tell us your reaction to the first column? Before and after my visit?"

A red-faced Gordon Rudge squirmed in his seat. "I felt sorry for my ex-wife. Through Jolene, I was aware of Elizabeth's struggles to regain her place in society. I thought the whole thing a sick revenge against her. You implied as much in your visit, Mr. Farina. It wasn't me. I didn't write the letter."

I knew Tiffany hadn't either but he didn't offer her innocence. I wasn't going to make it easy for him.

"Mr. Moore, you told me what you lost in your investments going sour. Would you give us a brief sketch and again tell us how the articles affected you?"

"I lost my house, my position and other luxuries. I didn't lose my family. With help from friends, I'm rebuilding, while learning what is important and what is not. *Stuff isn't.*" Armand spoke without rancour in his voice. He was one of those people who would survive. Observing and listening to him, I was glad he wasn't the culprit. "My reaction to the articles was sadness for others in my position who didn't have help."

"What made you invest with Mendez?" I asked.

"Greed. And I heard it as a hot tip. Rather, I overheard it being promoted. You hear something supposed to be in confidence and you place more value on it. I did."

I spoke before he could elaborate too soon. "That's enough for now, thanks, Mr. Moore. Oscar, you've been gracious and silent, would you care to comment on anything you've heard or are thinking?"

Oscar Jr. cleared his throat. "I'm silent through embarrassment. You know my reaction to the columns. A weak moment and anger at a family insult caused my scene at the newspaper office. My anger came from as much realizing the truth as reading it. I loved my father but I knew his weakness for winning. I inherited too much of that trait and take it out on the racetrack. I rarely win but I never get used to losing. The earthquake at the auction put a perspective on my father I didn't wish to recognize. When the ground began to shake, he looked to save himself first, leaving my mother alone. Business ethic shortcomings I could overlook, that character flaw revealed I could not. I lost my father two days ago." Oscar dropped his head for a moment. "I lost the father I respected long before."

The lump in my throat constricted my voice. I took a glass of water from the table to buy time. After a few moments, I had the confidence to speak firmly. "Oscar Jr. lost his father. Mr. Moore lost his house. The Rudges their Hawaiian retreat, their grand home, their friends and their social circle. These people's resilience inspires me.

"Let's return to the present." I took another swallow. Almost home. "Ms. Axford, can you comment on your weekend excursion?"

"I was approached by Mr. Mendez some time ago to be his agent for a revitalized project in Arizona." Colleen Axford spoke evenly without inflection. The sales persona had been left outside the room. Was she scared? "Despite what the letter writer may have thought, the California Securities people were close to pulling his license here. Arizona wasn't aligned with that; each state fiercely guards their right to make independent decisions around such matters. I flew to Phoenix to look at the development myself before signing an exclusive marketing arrangement with Mr. Mendez. I knew of his track record in California but this one looked like we could make it profitable for everyone, Mendez, me and our investors."

"When did you come back?" I asked.

"Monday afternoon."

"You didn't make an extra, private trip back and forth on Sunday?"

"No."

Oscar spoke again. "She didn't kill my father?"

"I had no reason to," said Axford. "I'm out of a deal."

Gordon spoke to Oscar Jr. "The letter writer killed your father. Indirectly."

I held up my hand to quiet the sudden chorus from a number of them. "It didn't, actually. I thought the same but Mr. Mendez's killing happened due to much more recent events, I believe."

Dennis' phone chirped and I watched him read the text. He gave me a nod.

"Oscar mentioned the earthquake reaction two weeks ago. I was there. I too witnessed Mendez Sr.'s character tell. There was another one I saw as well."

I took another deep sip. "Mr. Moore mentioned he had overheard a tip about the Mendez opportunity which tempted him. I'll ask him now to take up his story again, telling where he heard the tip." Time to put Moore to the test, see if he could convince the gathered.

"The Sea Grass Golf Club."

I saw Pops' hands grip the table.

"I was on the other side of a hedgerow from a group of guys. One in particular extolled a blue-ribbon opportunity. His company wasn't interested but he could get his guests on the president's list privately. I called my broker and we followed up on our own."

"Did you see the person?"

"I saw the foursome after the sales pitch but I didn't know which one of the four it was."

"But you'd recognize the voice again?"

"Yeah, very distinctive and burned into memory, given the subsequent financial disaster."

I moved to a position behind Pops. "I've got a character tell, a clandestine fund solicitor and a person who thought they were going to be Mendez's Arizona partners. Mendez betrayed that trust by signing with Ms. Axford on the weekend."

I stared across the table. "Milt, I guess it's time we heard from you. Tie it all together for us, would you?"

Milt Canyon looked up from his notes. It took him a long moment to compose a smile. "What are you talking about?" His levity was forced.

"Yours is the voice Armand Moore heard at the club. Farina-Black had a strict no-involvement policy when it came to Oscar Mendez. But you'd invested yourself and lost. Mendez convinced you the only way to gain back was to bring in other investors on commission. Your house is mortgaged for fifty percent more than it's worth. Your boat's for sale. Your wife's deserted you for Phoenix. You thought Mendez's new development would solve everything. If you could be his representative. Hell, my dad even offered to transfer you to Phoenix."

"Coincidence." Milt's veneer was beginning to crack but he wasn't down yet.

"When Mendez told you he'd signed with Axford, you returned here mad and desperate. You knew when and where he'd land. You hid in the shadows, waiting for him to get in his car. His shooting wasn't passion-fuelled. By the early hours on Monday morning, you'd cooled down to a rationale burn. You got into his car beside him. Closed your door and chatted for seconds, I'm guessing. You pressed the 9 mm pistol against his head and squeezed the trigger. Twice in quick succession."

Gasps and murmurs erupted.

"Quiet, please, people," called Dennis.

I continued the scene that I'd repeated many times in my head yesterday. "You got out of the car, donned a coverall and gloves. You drove to the marina, took your boat out to the middle of the bay and dumped your clothes and the gun overboard, weighed down with the boat's anchor. You returned to the marina when you knew there'd be a witness who'd assume you'd been out all night. You confirmed that with him, drove home, showered and came to work."

"Pretty imaginative, Clay." Milt glanced at Pops then back at me. "Come on, you know me."

"Not well, Milt. I watched you abandon your wife at the tremor's first shake at the auction. Like Mendez. Two of a kind. Anything you'd like to add, Sheriff Levi?"

Dennis stood. "We finished the search of his house and car. Found a box of 9 mm bullets in the garage. Flecks of blood on the car's headliner. From your hair, Mr. Canyon."

Milt pushed back his chair. Oscar Jr. launched himself across the table in a great tackle. Some screamed. Some got out of the way. Some tried to pull Junior off. I blocked the door. Roger and Pops pulled Oscar free and Dennis cuffed Milt. He was reciting his rights on the way out.

I closed the door behind them and leaned against it. A few of the attendees retook their seats while the others stood, unsure of what to do or say next.

Pops broke the silence. "Mendez was shot this time with a 9 mm? What about the .22 attack? Did Milt have more than one gun?"

I shook my head. "Milt didn't attack him the first time."

"Then who the hell did?" Pops asked.

I looked around the room. Dennis was gone but Colin Marsh the reporter remained. As did Roger Schopff, an officer of the court. "I have no idea," I said.

Epilogue

"**I** prefer full closure," said Pops.

"Dr. Wharton paid Buddy Tkachuk's hospital tab and the family has his remains." I swirled the wine. "I've got closure."

"I'm glad to hear Wharton's off your case but that isn't what I meant."

"I know. I was trying to divert."

"Clay found the murderer," said Ynez. "Isn't that closure?"

"We have an unknown shooter who attacked Oscar Mendez the first time." Pops paced on the veranda. He pointed his glass toward me. "I appreciate you didn't want to finger anyone while a reporter was in the room but now?"

"I don't know, Pops. Really." I didn't push Dennis to search any number of possible locations. The Mendez house, Jolene's ranch, Gordon and Tiffany's yacht. Just for starters. "There are too many people with motives and opportunity. Hell, it may not have been anyone in the room. I'll leave my peripheral board intact until I need it for the next case. Maybe the little ball will drop into the puzzle recess and reveal all. Colin Marsh and Dennis Levi have the same information as me, maybe one of them will put it together or find a fresh clue that draws the string tight. Does it matter? Mendez is dead. The Rudges and the Moore's can continue to rebuild their lives. I hope the Mendez's can start as well. I heard Colleen Axford is pounding the streets to keep the Phoenix project alive."

Pops nodded. "She'll do it. She has the stomach and the faith to get it done. I wish her luck."

"

Ynez picked up her purse from the tile and placed it on the patio table. "Should I?"

"Invest?" I asked. "What do you think, Pops?"

"I can give you half a dozen reasons on both sides. Come to the office and we'll discuss your time-line, risk tolerance and goals you may not have even considered."

Mom finally took charge. "No more business. You have exhausted the unfortunate Mr. Mendez's situation. Perhaps Ynez and I can talk about the university and its dark underside. Would that interest either of you?"

"You're right," said Pops.

"Mom, tell me there is no dark underbelly. Leave me one ray of hope." My board and my mind would keep filtering data until the next case overprinted. I glanced at Ynez's profile. Still stunning. She could overprint almost anything. I grabbed her hand. She smiled. Frontal view was as stunning as her profile.

The end

Also by Al Onia

Javenny

Transient City (Victor Stromboli 1)

Rogue Town(Victor Stromboli 2)

The Sixth Helix (Jake North Mystery 1)

The Fourth Vertex (Jake North Mystery 2)

The Third Redux (Jake North Mystery 3)

Barnacle Passage (Argosy Realm 1)

Shadowed Passage (Argosy Realm 2)

About the Author

Al Onia lives on Vancouver Island with his wife Sandra. Take Your Best Shot is his ninth published novel.

Read more at: ajonia.com